Cherished Illusions

Illusions

A NOVEL

SARAH STERN

Cherished Illusions

A NOVEL

Balfour Books

SARAH STERN

First printing: March 2005

ISBN: 0-89221-612-3

Library of Congress Control Number: 2004118185

Cover and interior design by Brent Spurlock, Green Forest, AR

Printed in the United States of America

Please visit our website for other great titles:
www.balfourbooks.net

For information regarding author interviews,
please contact the publicity department at (870) 438-5288.

In memory of my father, Bezalel Newberger, who has always been my yardstick with which to measure moral choices; of my mother, Ahuva Newberger who, had she had lived in a different time and place would have been able to actualize her potential and emerge from her cocoon into a beautiful butterfly; and to my sister Mynda Barenholtz, who with her eternal spirit of optimism taught me the value of seeing beyond the present to life's infinite possibilities.

And to Buddy, Bezalel, Noam, and Rachel, whose love has given me strength.

A human being is a part of a whole, called by us "universe," a part limited in time and space. He experiences himself, his thoughts and feelings, as something separate from the rest — a kind of optical delusion of his consciousness. This delusion is a kind of prison for us, restricting us to our personal decisions and to affection for a few persons nearest to us. Our task must be to free ourselves from this prison by widening our circle of compassion to embrace all living creatures and the whole nature in its beauty.

— Albert Einstein

CONTENTS

1. Separate Spheres 11

2. Intersecting Angles 19

3. Opaque Planes... 27

4. Opposing Angles 33

5. Divergent Paths 43

6. Refraction... 47

7. Static Forces.. 53

8. Prisms of Light 61

9. Shattered Fragments 69

10. Dissolution... 77

11. Free-floating Particles.. 83

12. Penetrating the Nucleus 89

13. Radiant Energy... 99

14. Fission 109

15. The Optical Microscope 119

16. Subatomic Particles.. 129

17. Inertia.. 135

18. Static Constants.. 141

19. Erosive Forces... 147

20. Particles of Light... 151

21. Luminesence... 159

22. Quantum Leaps... 163

23. Tenuous Equilibrium... 169

24. Natural Quirks 173

25. Infinite Universes.. 179

26. Mystic Constants.. 185

27. Toward a Unified Field Theory 187

    Epilogue 189

Chapter 1

SEPARATE
SPHERES

Alice: There's no use trying . . . one can't
believe impossible things.

The queen: I dare say you haven't had much practice.
Why sometimes I've believed as many as six
impossible things before breakfast.
— Lewis Carroll, *Alice in Wonderland*

It's very strange, how our lines intersect. We sometimes travel in
our separate spheres functioning under the delusions that the
boundaries between them are actually real . . . but I am getting
very much ahead of myself.

I first met Danielle when I was asked to supervise her
internship. I had been a psychologist working for a local school
system for many years, and she was reentering the work force
after many years as a homemaker. There was no doubt about it

— she was beautiful. A classic picture of refinement. She wore cultured pearls around her neck, 24-karat gold sculptured roses in her ears, and only the finest of fabrics, pure cotton, pure linen, pure silk, touched her perfectly proportioned body; so perfect, in fact that it seemed to have been divined by the gods as the platonic ideal of the feminine form. The perfect hourglass shape, long and slender, but voluptuous in just the right places.

She had been educated in the very best of schools, down to her prep boarding school. She always spoke in soft, lilting tones, and people found themselves straining to hear her voice. Her conversation was laced with lovely erudite or French expressions, such as "that's *a priori*" or "*au contraire*, which she would say while lifting her eyebrows as she spoke, portentously, as if to impart that she had an inside scope on some of the secrets of the universe, as though she understood much, much more about the world and its obscure mysteries, than the rest of us. On first impression, I was dwarfed with awe by this tall, wistful beauty with her fair hair and her perfectly chiseled features, the gentle patrician tilt to the nose, the sagacious arch to the eyebrows, the percipient highness of the forehead, the penetrating blue gaze. She would be coming to me, Rachel Stein, small, dark, and fragile in stature, for my guidance and support. She would be depending on my evaluation of her as a ticket to a new career, a new life. As time ensued, the irony of this situation became increasingly more obvious.

Little bits and snatches of Danielle's life began to gradually unfold. It soon became apparent that hers was a life on the rebound. She was in the midst of a sordid and very ugly divorce. For the very first time in her life, she had become aware that she might have to support herself and her family by her very own labors. Given this, she was quite fearful that even with the additional income of her employment, she would not be able to maintain the very high standard of living to which she had always been accustomed.

I, on the other hand, had simply not had the option not to work, until quite recently. It had been a simple matter of economic necessity. David and I had gotten married when we were quite young, and it takes many years to develop a medical practice. I was getting tired, at this point, of the continuous tug of war of the heart between the hearth and the office. Like so many other women of my generation, I was finding that the glitter of the women's movement was beginning to lose its luminescence at ten o'clock at night when you're at the check-out line in the grocery store, or when your child cries for you when you have to drop him off at the day care center. Things were just beginning to ease up now for us, financially, and I was beginning to contemplate cutting down on my hours, to spend time at home with my two young sons while they were still young enough to need me. I longed secretly for a daughter, as well. A little girl to take on the names of the grandmothers I had never met, but have heard so much about, and with whom I could develop that special, sweet, sisterly bond.

In contrast to Danielle, I had come from the very humblest of origins. My parents arrived here shortly after the war, with numbers on their arms and nightmares in their memories. I grew up in a small apartment, where hearts were much more abundantly furnished than rooms. Childhood, to me, meant summer time trips on the subway to Brighton Beach, Friday night meals with the family, after which they would tuck us into bed with wonderful stories about aunts and uncles and grandparents I never knew, who all had such wonderful qualities, who were so genuinely kind or good or God-fearing. These stories always had the same inevitable conclusion: "But then Hitler came . . ." and I was able to see that indelible pain and sadness that was so deeply etched across their gentle faces.

Still and all, the message was always the same: somehow goodness triumphed. After all, we were here . . . this was America . . . we have a new life now . . . we had survived. That I suppose, was their greatest legacy to me, this tenacity for life; this determination to perceive goodness and optimism and stamina, from this, among the cruelest and ugliest of chapters in human history — their sheer determination to be positive and sane, coming from a world that had been twisted and distorted and insane.

That is not to say that they didn't have their shares of nocturnal horrors. The horrors of their experiences in the past would come back to haunt them in the night, and I heard little snatches of this from the muffled cries of *"Nein . . . Bitte"* which would somehow creep their way past my bedroom door. But they so desperately tried to confine their horrors behind the locked doors of their bedroom. After all, they must have thought, we were children.

How could they bring children into such a world unless they opted to believe that there was sanity and justice? And at the very least, create that delusion for the children. How could they predicate their lives without such a premise, even if it was that, simply an act of faith, or a delusion?

So their screams remained muffled and their memories just shared between the two of them, like treasured marital intimacies. But still I knew . . . we all knew . . . by their tacit, gentle smiles and by their unspoken gestures, that lifting up of the shoulders and reaching outward of the palms, that they had witnessed too much of man's capacity for evil in their short lifetimes. Still, what they told us was that the path to Yad VaShem — Jerusalem' Holocaust museum — was planted with a groove in honor of the righteous Gentiles. The message was unspoken but clear: we can dwell on our wounds and focus on man's capacity for evil, or we can focus on those few heroes among us and marvel at their heroic capacity to do good. The choice is always ours . . . therefore choose life.

Still, as a little girl growing up in that household, I wanted so much to make it all up to them. I wanted to undo their bad memories, take away their headaches, protect them from any more pain. *What could I do, Daddy, Mommy, to make it up to you?* I often thought to myself. I fantasized about holidays and vacations spent with me, as an adult, that I would give them grandchildren to bounce on their knees and to take on their brothers' and sisters' names; that I would undo the horrors of their youth with pleasant golden years spent in my house with plenty of love and warmth and *"nachas."*

But biology was not so kind to me. I had difficulties conceiving and carrying babies to term. I had many unmourned babies aborted from my womb. Meanwhile, my father's body was slowly and painfully being ravaged by cancer. The time clock was steadily ticking away. . . . He never lived to see my childhood fantasies realized. I was pregnant with my oldest son when he died. The very day I got up from the *shiva* was the day I had an appointment with my obstetrician, and I heard my son Benyamen's heartbeat for the very first time. I remember laying on the examining table with tears steadily streaming down my eyes.

Shortly after that, my mother was stricken with Alzheimer's disease, often forgetting my name. The clock had definitely not waited for my fantasies to materialize.

Danielle's origins had been very different from mine. She had grown up right outside of Princeton, where her father had been employed as a physicist. She had known very few Jews as a child, with the exception of the children of a few of the mathematicians and physicists who worked there, but certainly no observant Jews.

Initially, she had kept many of the facts and details of her life as a tightly guarded secret. I knew that she had been raised as a Lutheran, and was sent to a high Episcopalian boarding school as a young girl. And I knew that, for some reason, a 24-karat gold Star of David now glistened delicately among the cultured pearls which Danielle wore around her neck. Danielle had told me that she had converted to Judaism. But what was the attraction of this ancient Semitic religion to this Gentile Nordic beauty who could enter with such ease into places restricted to Jews? Was it because her second husband had been

Jewish? But what had been the attraction there, to this aging
Semitic gynecologist? She had initially come to him as a doctor,
and he had committed the ultimate medical transgression: he
had slept with his patient. But had she not seduced him with
her gentle ways? Had the attraction been an oedipal one? Was
she sleeping with a father, the father with a history she would
have liked to have had? Was that what she wanted — to be
made love to by a Jewish father — a father with a history she
could design to her own liking?

We spent many hours together, initially. I saw in her a
great deal of promise, and felt that the time was well invested. I
taught her many of the more specific tricks of the trade, things
she would not learn in a graduate course — all sorts of devices,
metrics, and instruments which should help in making fair,
accurate, and valid diagnoses of children and the exact explana-
tion for why they were having difficulties in the classroom. My
leaning tended to be that of a scientist. "Always back up your
assessment with two or more instruments specifically designed
to diagnose that problem," I remember telling her. "When making a judgment on a child, always be sure to give the child the
benefit of the doubt. . . . Never let your subjective impressions
of the child cloud the picture. . . . Be extremely judicious and
careful about what you might say. . . . A label can follow a child
around for a lifetime."

By comparison with me, Danielle's leanings were those of
an artist. Even though she was quite inexperienced, she carried
with her the ease and confidence to be able to trust her basic
instincts, and to be able to make judgments of children with
an assuredness that I still lacked after so many years in practice.
(There was a certitude and grace about her insofar as her gut
feelings about children and the judgments involving them that
I found myself almost envious at times.) Even the enormous
responsibility of having to label a child as emotionally disturbed
did not seem to shake that ease. I had been practicing in this
field for over ten years now, and I still felt a bit of trepidation
about tracking youngsters into special programs based upon

their performance on the Rorschach or the Thematic Appercep-
tion Test, and always managed to lose more than a little bit of
sleep over it.

It seemed as though this confidence of hers was a gift from
childhood — either one had it or one didn't. There was hardly
any way of acquiring it as an adult. Somehow the weight of
any task didn't seem to affect her. Perhaps it was a birthright,
this ease of hers, having been born into a nobler social status.
While I had to equivocate and back up everything I said with
the data (and circles under my eyes), she spoke with panache
and awoke refreshed after eight hours of sleep. Why was I so
damned insecure about my findings, anyway? Was I just bogged
down by an overly empathetic and analytic perspective? Were
all those centuries of having been the underdog inhibiting my
ability to trust my instincts? Was this my struggling lower class
underpinnings showing through my facade as a professional?
How I envied Danielle for her legacy of *degagé* which gave her
the confidence to be a participant in life, while I was forever the
passive observer, doggedly recording all the data.

Occasionally, we would grab some time from our frenetic
schedules and manage to lunch over croissants and cappuccino
at a local patisserie. Although Danielle was now on a tight bud-
get, she would never deign to enter a McDonald's. If nothing
else, she had her standards. And the appearance of wealth was
something she would not easily relinquish. After all, she was a
Princeton thoroughbred. . . . She was pure . . . pure of breeding.
And all of this, all of this manner of *noblesse oblige*, seemed so
attractive and appealing to me, at the time.

If there was one thing Danielle lacked confidence about, it
was in working with what she called "a racially mixed" popu-
lation. She seemed reluctant to go into those schools, always
looking over her shoulder to make sure there wasn't some kin-
dergartner following her around the halls with an Uzi. She tried
to conceal it, but she did carry with her a certain disdain for the
lower classes, a kind of Ann Randian arrogance, as though these

children were in some way responsible for their parents' thin wallets. She did, at one point over our croissants and coffee, acknowledge that she would have difficulty accepting an assignment in a "racially mixed" area. "It is difficult," I responded while brushing croissant crumbs off my chin. The demands on professionals working with the poor are incredible. You have to be plugged into the whole social service network . . . be able to provide interpreters, sometimes attorneys who can find housing for the homeless — it's a whole different ball game, and often very draining."

"But how do you relate to them?"

"You mean can I find interpreters for every language, here? Well, not really." I paused to sip my coffee. "We have Hispanics, Vietnamese, Koreans, people from all over Africa . . . and then you have to start worrying about all the regional dialects."

"No, no. That's not what I mean." She seemed impatient. "Not how do you find interpreters . . . but how do you communicate with them? What's your common ground? What's your common denominator with those people?"

This annoyed me a little bit, this "those people" attitude of hers. But I assured myself that time and experience would make up for what she lacked in exposure as a child, in her princess-like childhood of Princeton. In the meantime, this did little to corrode my overall impression of enchantment for this ravishing beauty, so pure in breeding, who seemed to have glided into my life from the upper classes, like a visiting anthropologist just passing through . . . this Danielle Schoenfeld.

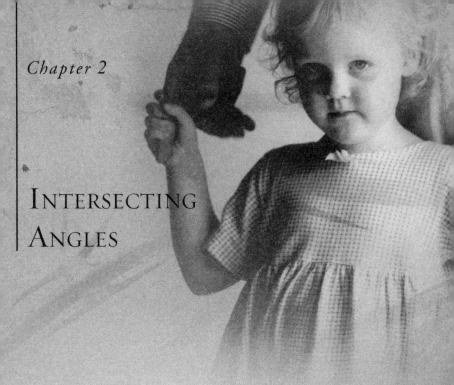

Chapter 2

INTERSECTING
ANGLES

Time it was, And what a time it was,
It was A time of innocence A time of confidences.
It was sweet
Long ago
I have a photograph
Preserve your memories
They're all that's left you.
— Paul Simon

It wasn't until about a month into the supervision that the cracks really began to emerge in Danielle's perfectly constructed veneer. It was just about the time that the Intifada began to emerge in Israel. Things were looking very bad for the little country, and I had to admit I was more than just a little bit concerned about how it would weather this, yet another crisis, in its young history. This tiny little state in the Middle East had always meant so much to me, as I know it had for many, to most Jews living in the Diaspora, and particularly for survivors and their families. It in no way offered a resolution to the six million, but yet it was something positive to cling to, a faint spark of light after such a dark and bitter history.

The background music of my childhood was the *"Hatik-vah,"* the song of hope, Israel's national anthem. And the only family I had left was my sister and her young family, who now were new settlers in the young West Bank settlement of Alon Shevut. I remember kissing them goodbye in the El Al terminal in New York, and holding my beautiful blond nephew, Amir, very close to me, silently praying that he would not be yet another name in an endless casualty list, in what seemed like an eternal, atavistic conflict. I was afraid that the sweet strains of the flutist were soon to be drowned out by a chorus of primitive, tribal chants.

I remember how Rivka, my beautiful sister, with her long auburn hair tied under a dark forest green kerchief, looked at me with such understanding in her penetrating hazel eyes, and said, *"Iyeh Beseder"* (It will be all right). She took my hand firmly and said, "It's something I've gotta do. . . . Israel is the stage, the only stage where the drama of Jewish history continues . . . where the thread of our people will endure." (I was crying, silently now. Why? Because of my loss?) "You have to understand, Rach," she said while squeezing my hand gently in hers, "I've got to continue the dream."

That was about two years ago. Since then, Elona has appeared on the scene, a beautiful seven pound, five ounce niece, whom I regularly get snapshots of in the mail. I must have said a million silent prayers for their safety in this tumultuous parcel of earth that somehow has become the metaphysical heart valve to so many diverse peoples. And so, I had become obsessed with the news. I no longer woke up to the beautiful strains of Bach or Mozart on WGMS, our local classical station, but to the sobering reports on WRC, the news station. And like every other good self-flagellating Jewish liberal, I was holding my people's actions up against a perfect moral yardstick, examining it in the cold light of objective, ethical scrutiny, while I was so, so far away from the hub of these passions and their rock-throwing and Uzi-carrying children. Still, I shivered over this fragile, diminutive slip of land, and its continuous existence. One thing our people's recent history had taught me: our enemies mean business.

At about this time, Danielle invited me to her home. It was the perfect pristine setting for her, very well situated in upper Georgetown, an ivy-coated brick brownstone with black shutters and brass accents. Inside the entrance way were Italian marble floors and a hand-crafted oak banister gracing a spiral staircase. The living room was richly appointed with an ebony Steinway baby grand piano, dark oak parquet floors on which lay rich Persian carpets, Italian white leather sofas, a dramatic white marble, oval-shaped fireplace, and french windows overlooking an enclosed garden, beautifully landscaped in rich autumn hues, scarlet, canary yellow and mandarin orange chrysanthemums and burnt carmine and golden yellow marigolds. Above the fireplace hung an oil painting of a beautiful Georgian estate which Danielle later told me was her childhood home. And this, this was just the perfect setting for my new beautiful intern with all her polish and refinement. The only element that was slightly out of character were the New Year's cards, marking the start of the Jewish New Year, which she left incongruously dangling over the marble fireplace. It was not just their fragility that seemed to clash with everything else around, which all seemed so sturdy and eternal, it was the fact that this was mid-November, and the Jewish New Year takes place in September. Was this, as good old Freud would have had it, a subconsciously intentional action with an accompanying statement, or merely an act of omission in a busy life on the rebound? Why was I always so analytical about everything? Couldn't I ever take anything just at face-value, and take off my psychoanalytic glasses?

Danielle served a simple but elegant lunch, salad nicoise on lovely Steuben crystal bowls, out of consideration for me, because I maintained the laws of Kashruth. All of this about me, Danielle seemed to find particularly intriguing, perhaps, I reasoned, because she had never known any observant Jews before. I also noticed that when she mentioned her friends with Jewish surnames, she had a manner of exaggerating the syllables, as if to flaunt her friendship with them, as though she were saying "Rockefeller" or "Kennedy," when she actually said "Goldberg" or "Cohen."

Although Danielle had converted to Judaism, she did not maintain many of the traditions. When I asked why she converted, she staunchly maintained, "It wasn't because of Eric. I didn't do it because of any man. It was something I always wanted to do, for . . . philosophical reasons. I just always knew deep inside myself that I was meant to be a Jew."

It was one of those Indian summer, sun-drenched afternoons when everything seems so right with the world. Particularly, with this little corner of the world, this world of Danielle's. Everything seemed so authentic, so genuine. Everything was of the absolute finest quality, from her Steinway piano to her Steuben bowls. Even her act of becoming a Jew seemed to me to be so authentic. It was an act of genuine conviction, of conscious, deliberate choice, carefully thought out, as opposed to having been perfunctorily bestowed upon one at birth. Nothing here rang ersatz or false; everything genuine and pure.

After lunch, we both retired to the living room where Vivaldi's "The Seasons" was softly playing on the compact disk. We were both happy and relaxed, slightly high.

"Tell me about your childhood," Danielle said, raising her eyebrows with interest, as she so often did.

"There isn't much to say. It wasn't a particularly impressive childhood."

"Where did you grow up?"

"In Westchester — but don't get the wrong idea — it was definitely on the wrong side of the tracks." (We both exchanged little chuckles.)

"What did your father do?"

"He was a cantor in a synagogue."

"That's all he did?"

"Well, no, he taught — mostly Bar Mitzvah lessons, sometimes Hebrew."

"So you must have been pretty poor?"

"Well, not actually. That is, on paper, our income wasn't very impressive, but I never actually felt poor. It's just that I thought everyone else in Westchester was rich." (We both laughed again.)

She kicked off her shoes, and put her feet up on the soft leather sofa. "So your father was a cantor? Tell me. How does one cant? Where does one learn to be a cantor? Are there colleges in the United States that teach that? Do you major in "cantoring" in Divinity School?"

There was something about her manner now that distinctly annoyed me, a slight smugness underneath her mild interest. She half sucked in her words as she spoke, as only someone who hails from Princeton or environs knows how to do.

"No, it wasn't like that at all. My father had his *"smicha"* his rabbinical degree, at a very young age. He was also studying for his Ph.D. in German philosophy and literature before the war at the University of Heidelberg. But after the war, he never wanted to speak the language again."

A certain ashen quality rose in her face. "And why didn't he use his rabbinical degree?"

"Well, he was in a rush to start his life over again. He arrived in this country hardly knowing any English. He was a little self-conscious to take on a pulpit, and he was anxious to start a family, again, to re-create a life for himself. He was offered this position, and though it didn't pay much, it was secure — and I guess that's what he needed at the time."

"But he wasn't in the camps, was he?"

"He spent six years in them — six miserable, forgotten years."

"And your mother, your mother's American?"

"No, my mother also spent six years, first in hiding, then in the *Przemysl* forced labor camp, and later in Auschwitz . . . Birkenau . . . the women's section."

"Where did they meet?"

"In a displaced person's camp, after the war. They married shortly after that. They were anxious to restart their lives. By the time my parents arrived on these shores, my mother was pregnant with my older sister, Rivka."

Danielle got up to change the compact disk. When she returned, her mood was much less buoyant, more reflective, somber.

"Rachel," she said, "I have something to tell you. My father was a member of Hitler Youth. I'm not exactly sure of the story. All I know is that it was like joining the boy scouts in that day and age. Everybody did it. He came from a very aristocratic military family in Germany. Everyone had military honors in his family tree. I don't know what all of his relatives were doing during the war, and I don't care to know. But my father acted heroically. That I am sure of."

"Really? How?"

"I'm not really sure, but this I know. His hands were clean. Pure. He was trained in the very best military schools in Germany at the time, was educated to be a physicist and an engineer. But he escaped the Hitler war machine. He never did a single thing to any Jew."

I was intrigued, not really comprehending what I was hearing. "How did he do that?"

"He sacrificed tremendously. He came to this country, and worked as a plumber during the war years, even though he had received the finest education. He gave up everything for his ideals. He was a noble man — a very noble man. He walked away from it all."

"That's fantastic. How did he manage to get out? When did he come?"

"I don't know how he managed to get out. I'm sure, heroically, somehow, and at great personal sacrifice. But I know he arrived here in 1945."

Suddenly a distinct wave of nausea overcame me. 1945! Didn't she know the war was over by then? Either she had her dates all wrong (Could it have been *1935*? One digit could make all the difference!), or what she was believing about this man was a delusion. If she was going to believe all this stuff, she should at least get her chronology straight!

"Rachel," her voice was droning on, softly, "I miss him so much, now. He's been dead for four years. I really consider myself fortunate. I had a wonderful father. Wonderful. Not everyone could say the same thing about their dads. At least it was good while it lasted."

It was too much for me to digest at once. There we were, two daughters still longing for our dead fathers. How could I tell her that this father she was mourning for, this noble hero, possibly never existed? How could I tell her what I suspected — that this man was probably not an idealist, and was possibly a murderer? She had so much, so much invested in this illusion, and he was dead and buried. What did it matter? Does the truth enter in here? Should it? Would it bring back my grandparents? Would it undo my parents' suffering? I was confused, and sickened. I closed my eyes, and in a flash pictured a featureless Nazi stuffing thousands of Jews into a cattle car. Could that Nazi have been her father? Could one of those Jews have been mine? The bile was swelling up my throat now.

Suddenly I excused myself, telling Danielle that the children would be arriving home from school soon. I darted out the front door. This little world of Danielle's which had seemed so perfect, so pristine, just a few moments ago, suddenly seemed so tainted, so ersatz, so false. It was a delusion. I knew that from the bottom of my very being. Just as I knew the numbers on my parents arms. But this? This physicist turned plumber turned owner of a Princetonian manner overnight? This . . . I just couldn't swallow. The bile was coming up now. I had to rush very, very quickly. I threw up all over her beautiful autumn chrysanthemums, before I had a chance to make it to the car.

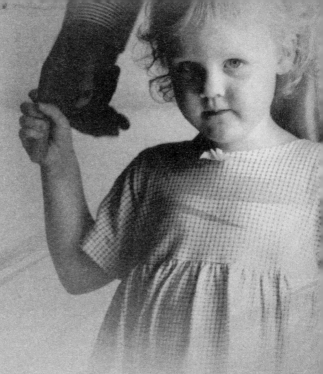

Chapter 3

Opaque
Planes

Perhaps it's the color of the sun caught flat
uncovering the crossroads I'm standing at. . . .
Or maybe its the weather . . . or something like that. . . .
But daddy . . . you've been on my mind.
— Bob Dylan

We who knew our fathers in everything, in nothing.
They perish. They cannot be brought back.
The secret worlds are not regenerated. And every time again
and again I make my lament against destruction.
— Yevgeny Alexandrovich Yevtushenko, "People"

The drive back through Rock Creek Park was a difficult one
for me. One of those unpredictable and chilling mid-autumn
rain storms suddenly emerged, fogging up my windshield and
clouding my perspective. Everything seemed so suddenly murky
and confused. There was a constant throbbing pain at the side

of my head. How I recognized that voice of Danielle's. I've heard it often enough in myself. I know that deep, that stabbing anguish that only a daughter can have for her dead father. I know of that void, that place in the heart that will forever lie dormant . . . of that furtive search for paternal substitutes to fill it up, and of that final, painful recognition that there will be no substitute — that that organ of your body will be permanently vacant in that special artery that had once been filled up with the life-sustaining force that only a father's love can provide.

I know, Danielle, I know of that irreparable tear of the fragile strings of the heart. And I know that this father bounced you on his knee and played horsy with you and showered you with Christmas and birthday presents in brightly wrapped packages and with love and affection. But I also know that this father that you loved, this heroic idealist, was either an illusion or a delusion. His hands might well have been dripping with my grandparents' blood.

By the time I pulled into my driveway, I had worked myself up into one of my full-scale migraine headaches. I turned off the ignition, and a few minutes later climbed into bed to try to exorcise the headache and these thoughts from my mind, at least until the kids got home from school.

That night was a sleepless one. I tossed and turned trying to find a comfortable spot on the bed, to hide from the demons that were haunting me throughout the night. I couldn't escape my tormenting curiosity which kept bringing me back 40 years or so to Berlin. What was this man then? Was he merely an enlisted man, sent off to the Russian front, conscripted into the Luftwaffe against his will? Was he a guard in a concentration camp? Was he responsible for some of the infamous "experiments" on the prisoners or selections or deportations? Was he a Gestapo or SS man?

I closed my eyes in a half dream-like state, and envisioned a Jewish family in Berlin coming home from services. It was Erev Rosh Hashana, one of the holiest evenings in the year.

The children were dressed in their very best. There was a white tablecloth on the table, sparkling silver candlesticks, flowers. A little boy, about four or five years old with glistening dark locks and pink cheeks stood to recite the *kiddush*. All of a sudden, the dream is shattered by a group of Nazi Gestapo agents bursting in, and rounding up the family in the middle of the street with hundreds of other Jews for deportations. In my half-dream state I caught a glimpse of the face of one of the Gestapo agents. I recoiled in terror, realizing I recognized that face. It was simply Danielle's, in the male form. Or had he actually been an inmate in one of the concentration camps, a fellow prisoner with my parents, a conscientious objector? Was there some part of the story that Danielle believed that was based on the truth? Or was it all true? Had her father protected her, just as mine had tried to, from the nightmare of those years? Perhaps he had sacrificed a great deal for his ideals, but had he spared her the horrors of the circumstances he had to endure for those ideals, out of fatherly love, just as mine had?

Or perhaps her father had actually been a Nazi war criminal, the lowest of the low, who managed to slip into this country by assuming an alias, probably a Jewish surname, as so many others had? Maybe what Danielle believed was based on the stories he himself had told her. Maybe it was not a delusion of her own invention, but simply an illusion he presented to his precious little girl, so that he could continue to be the untarnished apple of her eye, her white knight in shining armor, perfect and pure?

These questions were tormenting me, incessantly, throughout the night, robbing me of my precious sleep. I turned and looked over at David, sleeping on the other side of the bed, his chest rising and falling, so rhythmically — so stable and solid, just as he had always been for me since the moment I met him 16 years ago in Jerusalem. That was the time when Israel had been in its heyday, those heady, wonderful days after the 1967 War, and before the Yom Kippur War. Everything had seemed so just, so right with the world, so free from any ambiguities, and I knew after the second sentence we had exchanged that this person would be right for me. Something intuitive inside of me knew this person would always be available to lean on and to share with. And I have never been wrong about that.

But now I was jealous of him in his peaceful slumber, while this insomnia was driving me nuts. I submitted to my more baser impulses and woke him up.

"Dave," I said.

No response.

"Dave," I said again (as though there were a fire raging throughout the bedroom).

He awoke with a start. "What's wrong, Rach?"

"Dave, I have something to tell you. . . ."

"Now? At four o'clock in the morning?"

"It's about Danielle."

He turned around, his back to me, and put the pillow over his head. I continued talking, as though I had his full, absorbed attention (an acquired skill . . . it comes with being a wife).

"It's about her father," I continued on. "It's very suspicious. Something tells me he might have been a Nazi."

Now I got his attention. He took the pillow off his head and turned toward me. "How do you know that, Rach?"

"I don't know it. It's just that the story she told me about him just doesn't hang together right."

He sat up in bed, and lifted the covers off his chest. "What did she say about him?"

"Well, that he was born in Germany, came from a military family, went to the very best military schools, was a member of Hitler Youth."

"Doesn't sound too promising."

"Yeah. But she also told me he was trained as an engineer and physicist before the war, but escaped Hitler's war machine, managed to get to this country, and worked as a plumber."

"Well, it doesn't sound very plausible . . . but it's possible. Anything is possible. Those times were so twisted and bizarre. But I'm sure if he was so highly educated and skilled the Third Reich would not have been so willing to relinquish him. Sounds unlikely, but who knows? Not me, especially not at four o'clock in the morning. What year did she say he got out?"

"That's just it, Dave. She said he came over here in 1945."

"The war was over in 1945, Rach."

"I know. I hope I'll be able to work with her the rest of the year. I just can't stand not knowing the truth about him."

"So what if her father was a Nazi? There are plenty of ex-Nazis running around today. One of them might happen to be the chancellor of Austria."

"It's more than that, Dave. It's that she believes he was a totally honorable man . . . a hero . . . an idealist."

"An idealist who helped to make Europe Judenrein?"

"No, no, no. She believes he took part in none of that . . . at great personal sacrifice."

"Is he alive?"

"Dead."

"You'll never know, Rach — for the 50th time, you won't solve all the world's problems at four o'clock in the morning. Go to sleep."

But of course I didn't. I was worried that I would not be able to give Danielle objective supervision for the remainder of the year. I was concerned that I might be biased. Would I be able to interact with her freely, naturally again? Would I be able to even look her in the face again without being haunted by an image of the cattle cars or of that horrible Nazi face that glared at me in my half-sleep? Would I subconsciously be punishing her for the sins of her father . . . real or imagined?

At about six in the morning, I finally did drift off to sleep. I dreamt I was a little bubble floating freely and innocently in the sunshine over a verdant meadow, refracting the light of the sunshine in my purity. All of a sudden I collided with another bubble — a brown, murky, ugly bubble. We intercepted, then burst — polluting the universe all around us with a muddy, vile fluid. I awoke feeling tainted, filthy, soiled; and quickly ran into the shower to cleanse myself.

Chapter 4

Opposing Angles

Anyone desiring a quiet life has done badly
to be born in the 20th century.
— Leon Trotsky

Oh, it is sad, very sad, that once more, for the umpteenth time,
the old truth is confirmed: "What one Christian does is his
responsibility, what one Jew does is thrown back to all Jews."
— Anne Frank, *The Diary of a Young Girl*

In the morning, Danielle and I reached the office at about the
same time. I was determined to carry about an air of normalcy,
and was more than a little bit concerned that Danielle might
have read my mind the previous afternoon and detected my
suspicions about her father, or perhaps she had caught a whiff
of the chrysanthemums.

We walked to the coffee maker together, as was our morning ritual, trying to "get the cobwebs out of our heads," as we

often put it, before we faced the day. I was able to detect from Danielle's manner almost immediately that something was bothering her. I reached for her cup, and began to slowly pour her coffee.

"Cream?" I asked, casually.

"Just black."

"How are you, today?" I asked, cautiously.

"Well frankly . . . slightly miffed."

(*Uh oh*, I thought to myself, she had noticed the mums.) "What's wrong, Danielle?" I asked, somewhat warily.

"It's this lunacy with Israel. Every time I turn on the news, I hear another report about the Intifada. I'm sick of seeing these reports of brutality by Israeli soldiers."

"I know. It's awful"

"What is it with these people? I'm beginning to feel so disgusted I think that I just might . . . I don't know."

"Well it's not all 'these people.' Every country has their few extremists, their few fanatics. Desperate situations sometimes make for desperate solutions. But these people who are doing brutal acts, they're not at all representative of the entire nation of Israel, and I'm certain that they'll be brought to justice. No one endorses this sort of behavior."

"What do you mean, 'No one endorses this sort of behavior?' Isn't the government sending soldiers into the occupied territories? These Palestinians are desperate for a homeland. And all they have are rocks and stones against the Israeli soldiers with their sophisticated weapons. They're just children!" Her voice was raised in disgust above the usual hushed tones found around an office coffee maker. I noticed some people turning around to stare at us, and was beginning to feel slightly uncomfortable.

"Wait a minute, Danielle," I said, trying to maintain as cool and relaxed a tone as possible. "These are not just a few defenseless children throwing snowballs against an army. This is a well-organized force. These people are throwing huge stones and molotov cocktails, fire-bombing cars against civilians who are just on their way to and from school or work. They mean business. They want Jerusalem. They want Haifa. They want Tel Aviv. They don't want a piece of it — they want it all. They want the Jews out of there."

Why were we getting into this? I asked myself. It's too early in the morning, and I haven't had my second cup of coffee yet. It's so complicated, more complicated than I had the energy to delve into this early in the day. Why were we choosing up sides? Is this the way of the world? Is there some ontological necessity to place ourselves in these neat little ideological categories, our separate spheres, which are usually determined by ascription — white/black, Christian/Jew, Arab/Israeli. . . .

Must all of our opinions and attitudes follow suit, as if we were acting out some words on a script that was given to us at the delivery table? And here I was, doing it, just like in the Middle East.

"How do you know that?" Danielle continued. "How do you know that if the Palestinians got their own state, they wouldn't be content to sit peacefully at Israel's borders?"

"I know that because I read the newspapers. The P.L.O. adopted a "phased plan" policy in Cairo in 1974. This plan calls for several phases to achieve the total destruction of the state of Israel. The first phase is going to be a "peace offensive" to win the support of the Western world. The second stage calls for the establishment of a P.L.O. state on any of the occupied territories that Israel chooses to give back. The third stage calls for the use of this state as a base for the "armed struggle," thus touching off a war on Israel's borders in which the Arab states will annihilate a smaller, more vulnerable state."

"How do you know that they really aim to annihilate Israel? How do you know that once they got their own state, they wouldn't just want to coexist peacefully?"

"It says so in the P.L.O. Charter, which calls for the destruction of the state of Israel. Article 19 of the charter says the existence of Israel is "null and void." If the P.L.O. were to embark on any peace initiative, the 'phased plan' will lay at the heart of their political strategy. It is all clearly set forth in the newspapers in Arabic. I know it because Sheik Abdel Hamid Sayeh, head of the P.L.O's Palestine National Council, said it: 'We want the whole of Palestine.' " Many others say the same thing.

"And what if they were to embark on a peace initiative? Couldn't we give them the benefit of the doubt?"

"What they say before the United Nations or to Western countries and what they say among themselves are totally different things. They have neither a free press nor a democratic electorate to answer to. If they are really so interested in peace, let the P.L.O dismantle the terrorist component of the organization. Let them stop bombing innocent civilians."

"But why must the Israelis, as people, be so militaristic? So aggressive?"

"Danielle, its very complicated," I said, stirring my coffee slowly with a spoon. "You have to understand that Israel was born at about the time of the emergence of worldwide nationalism, including Arab nationalism. Adolf Hitler actually met with the Grand Mufti of Jerusalem in 1941 to spread his creed of anti-Semitism, and to make sure that his job would be finished off in that corner of the world. In other words, to make the Middle East as Judenrein as Europe. About the only thing that unites the very feuding and divisive Moslem world is the notion that they want the Jews out of there."

"Yes. And the Israelis aren't nationalistic?"

"I'm not saying that, but they've fought four wars, all in self-defense, and would still be at war if their Arab neighbors thought there was any chance of defeating her and 'driving her into the sea.' We're talking about survival, here. You have to understand the type of neighborhood in which they live. We're not talking about hyphenated American neighbors here, like Italian-American, or Irish-American neighbors. The salient words to remember here are 'Hama,' the town where Syria dealt with its Islamic uprising by killing approximately 20,000 people in two weeks, and then paving over the dead, and 'Black September,' the period in 1970 when Jordan dealt with its Palestinian prob-lem by killing at least 2,500 people in ten days. These people mean business."

"Let me tell you something, Rachel. No person has the right to pick up a weapon against any other human being. I told my children that if they are in Hebrew school, and their teachers ever talk to them about taking another person's life in self-defense, they are to get themselves up, and walk out of there. This is definitely not what I converted to Judaism for."

This is not what she converted to Judaism for, I said to my-self. She'd prefer us still walking passively to the gas chambers? Possibly designed and operated by one of her kin . . . if not her cherished father? How quaint our bodies of skeletons would have looked piled up in Auschwitz.

She went on, with the blind veneer of an ideologue, "Let me tell you something else, Rachel. Last Saturday, I took my children to temple. And the rabbi started going on about Israel's recent actions. He quoted Golda Meir when she said, 'We can forgive the Arabs for many things, but not for making soldiers out of our children.' Well, I picked myself up and got my chil-dren up, and I marched out of there."

"But it's true. The reality of the situation is. . . ."

"You can change the reality of the situation if everyone puts down his gun. It says in the Torah that human life is the most sacred thing."

"It also prohibits suicide in the Torah!" *Who was she,* I thought, *quoting my Torah to me. This Aryan princess?*

"And what if your neighbors don't buy into the same beauti-ful, pacifist philosophy," I continued. "As they're about to drive you into the sea, do you think they're going to sit down and have a nice little philosophical chat with you?"

"Listen, Rachel," she said while lifting her eyebrows in that way that of hers, as though she were imparting one of the universe's eternal truths, "I've taught my children that no person has to lift a gun up against another person. If there is one thing they have to be proud of it's their grandfather's legacy of pacifism. No one had more at risk than he, but he walked away. He walked away from it all, under the most extreme conditions in Nazi Germany."

That nausea, so familiar to me by now, was beginning to come back again. I was numbed. Suddenly, I felt something ugly stirring up inside me. Was it hatred . . . or disgust? Who was this person with her sacrosanct words, so far from the reality of the situation? And moreover, who was this father, this paradigm of virtue, this standard of morality that she uses to measure all of humanity and their actions up against? And what was he doing in Nazi Germany until 1945? Preaching his gospel of passive resistance to the children of Hitler Youth — to Goebbels, to Himmler, to Goering, or perhaps to the Führer, himself?

Why couldn't I just ask her what he was doing in the Third Reich all those years? Why couldn't I bring myself to tell her that the war ended in 1945 — the very year he arrived on these shores? I couldn't. I simply couldn't do this to her. I couldn't shatter her cherished illusion.

The strength was beginning to drain away from me. I could almost feel it oozing out of my fingers.

"You know," I said in a very soft voice, "speaking of Nazi Germany — Israel was built on the ashes of the Holocaust." (I said this as though I was revealing some deep, dark family secret.)

She looked at me as though I was reminding her of some annoying little pain — some vexing, epispastic thorn in her backside. "Listen, Rachel. I'm sick of hearing about the Holocaust. Everybody's sick of it." (She had an unattractive, obdurate quality to her face, now.) "Don't you understand," she went on, "the Holocaust is passé now? The birth of Israel is old hat? There is a new drama in the Middle East that has replaced that old story . . . that story of 'out of the ashes of the Holocaust' that we've all heard on and on ad nauseam. The new story of the valiant struggle of the Palestinians for their homeland."

I really was speechless, now. The coffee, poured long ago, was now cold in my cup. *Is this all that mattered?* I thought to myself. *What was the latest vogue? Like some Seventh Avenue designers allured by the latest fashions walking down some Parisian runway ? The struggle that has happened to capture the public's imagination, of a people overcoming a brutal occupation in their struggle for freedom, suddenly carried with it more moral weight? The other story becomes like an old scratched record, whose melody you've heard too much — it grates on your nerves, and is doomed to be forever shelved and forgotten. Is that going to be the fate of the Hatikvah that I love so much?*

I suddenly felt numb, thinking of the one and a half million children who silently marched to their deaths in Auschwitz, who were buried in unmarked graves somewhere in Europe, by her people. Were their deaths, too, passé? Did they also warrant being shelved from the public's consciousness forever, gathering dust in some remote corner of one's memory?

Is this also how news stories are reported? One's point of view depends on what has suddenly captured the journalist's attention? He focuses his camera's lens on this piece of it, and eliminates all else, because this focus presents a novel twist, suddenly interesting to the public's imagination? He has no time to zoom his camera's lens on the other facts, as compelling as they might be, if he or the public is bored of it, like a monotonous old refrain on a broken record?

And is that somehow how we get our view of "the Truth"? Our journalist's impressions become recorded in our history books, and it becomes an illusion of "the Truth" that we all believe? Like a Bible story or a fairy tale told by a father to his little girl? Never questioned. Swallowed whole, and taken in, in perfect faith?

"But Danielle," I said, "you were the one who first mentioned Nazi Germany. . . ."

"Yes," she interrupted me, "because my father did not have to suffer. He was not a Jew."

I see — that says it all. Jews are supposed to suffer. But we don't want to be reminded of it. That's their rightful place in the history books — oppression, ghettos, humiliation, banishments, showers, and gas chambers. And how dare they try to escape from their rightful place with this vexing little state in the Middle East?

"Danielle," I finally said very meekly, suddenly thinking of my beautiful nephew Amir with his golden locks, and having the sudden strong desire to whisk him off and take him away from this fire, from the seat of this interminable conflict, and just nurture him and rock him and hug him. "Danielle," I repeated, "where are the Jews supposed to go?"

"I don't know," she said with a little shrug, as though I was asking her some trivial little fact, like the capital of Bhutan. "Back to where they came from, I guess."

How could I tell her that "back to where they came from" was the concentration camps, designed, owned, engineered, and operated by her people to my people? I couldn't. I simply couldn't, and remained mute.

That night I dreamt a strange dream. I was a Jewish woman in Europe. After a three-day train trip on a sealed freight train, squeezed together with 3,000 other Jews, I arrived under the gates of Auschwitz. I was carrying my baby, Raizel, under my arms. A Nazi tried to grab her, but my grasp was tighter. I wouldn't let her go. He sneered as though he knew he had "the final laugh" and directed me to go "to the right," where a group of female Nazi officers ordered us to strip down to our skin. They shaved our heads, and paraded us in front of a group of jeering Nazis. They ordered us to dig a ditch. We knew it was to be our grave. I heard some women davening softly to themselves, and mumbling *"Shema Yisroel."* I shielded Raizel's eyes with my hands from the ugly sight of the jeering Nazis with their machine guns. I overheard one officer saying to another, "These Jews. They deserve it," he laughed. "They're just so damned passive."

The scene shifts. I'm in Israel now, with my baby, Raizel. We live in Elon Moreh, a settlement on the West Bank. We are going together to Jerusalem in an EGGED bus where we will meet my husband, David, who is on leave from the army for Shabbat. Raizel is dressed up in a pretty, white dress for Shabbat. We have to take Derech Hevron, the road through Hebron — there is no other route. Suddenly, a group of young Arabs block the road with tires ignited by gasoline. They throw stones at our EGGED bus. The window next to Raizel suddenly shatters. An amalgam of glass and stone falls through the window, landing on Raizel's eye, cutting through the cornea. The blood spills all over, running down her beautiful face, spilling all over her white Shabbat dress. A journalist watches the scene and transmits it via satellite to the United States. In living rooms throughout this country, people watching it on their TVs, complacently lift their legs up on their reclining chairs, and mutter to themselves, "These Jews. They deserve it. They're just so aggressive and militaristic."

I awoke in a cold sweat. Our people knew nothing but passivity for 2,000 years, while her people called us *lebensunwurdiges* (life unworthy of life). The words on my people's lips were *Ahavat HaShem* (love of God) and *Tikun Olam* (the healing of the world through moral acts), while the words on her peoples' lips were *Einsatzgruppen* (rounding up Jews and killing them in mass standings) and "Project Reinhardt" (confiscating Jewish money and properties for the Aryan race).

Her people painfully taught my people, through difficult lessons, the necessity of incorporating words like Uzi and

Mossad into our vocabulary. And now, she calls us too "aggressive" and "militaristic."

The Nazi propaganda pamphlets of the 1930s must have known a deeper truth when they wrote, addressing German women, "Your body does not really belong to you, but to your brethren and to your Volk." I shivered, drawing up the covers around myself. Danielle's family in Germany were anti-Semites. Danielle is an anti-Zionist. They are merely just mutations of the very same animal.

Chapter 5

DIVERGENT
PATHS

One common characteristic of all such
(deterministic or teleological) outlooks is the
implication that the individual's freedom of
choice . . . is ultimately an illusion.
— Isaiah Berlin in *Historical Inevitability*

After that, I spent a great deal of time trying to avoid Danielle.
I told her that I thought she was ready to go out into the field
on her own now, partly because I felt she really was, and partly
because I was confused about my own feelings regarding her. I
certainly didn't appreciate this new emotion she elicited within
me, this ugly bile churning in my stomach, that I tried so
desperately to ignore. So I told her, with the proud smile of a
parent during a child's graduation, that I had given her about as
much as I had to offer, that she had wings now, and was ready
to fly, and that, for the duration of the year, we would be "like
ships passing in the night."

No long after our little conversation, I remember slipping out of the office a half hour early to treat myself to what I knew was the well-deserved luxury of a manicure. The manicurist I had was a beautiful Persian woman who had recently fled Iran, after the shah was deposed, with her young husband, leaving behind her family. The newspapers that week had been screaming with the headlines of Saddam Hussein of Iraq's use of poisonous nerve gas on Kurdish villages in Iraq. Her country was at war with Iraq, and if he can use poison chemicals on his own citizens, who knows what he can do to a sworn national enemy? It had been weeks since she had heard from her family, and, of course, she was quite worried.

Her words suddenly evoked such a tremendous mixture of empathy and pathos within me. Somehow, it couldn't have mattered less that my grandfather had been poring over the Torah while her grandfather had been poring over the Koran. What mattered was this poor woman's concern over the people she loved, and their fate in the hands of some Sunni Moslem fanatics, not so different at all from the concern my parents had had over the fate of their parents at the hands of some Nazi fanatics. As she massaged lotion into my chapped hands, I suddenly felt a warm bond with this person, that transcended our very distinct spheres of ascription, which somehow seemed so much more real to me than those neat little ontological packages that everyone always seems to want to put each other into.

My momentary warm, empathic spell was, however, soon to be broken by the brash voice of an over-bleached, over-permed Yuppie in a snit. She was clothed in a tight, white sweatshirt, glitzed up with rhinestones and little pink bows, form-fitting jeans (which were probably designed for someone half her age, and which were washed out in just the right places), pink socks and white sneakers, also with the added touch of rhinestones, and pink shoelaces carefully laced up on half of the holes for her shoelaces (obviously the latest fashion trend out of Candy Land).

"Fallah," she said in an urgent, whiny voice to my manicurist, "I don't know what I'm going to do. We have a very important dinner party tonight, and two of my acrylic nails fell off."

Now this, I thought to myself, *this constitutes a real emergency. Who cares if your loved ones are lying dead in some Persian village, at the mercy of some Islamic zealots. A broken nail, not to mention two . . . now that is a matter of supreme urgency.*

The desperate over-frizzed Yuppie brandished her hand on the table, as though she was returning home from the battlefield, revealing her wounds for the first time to a loved one. Fallah immediately sensed the dire urgency of the situation and began work at once on her bright, fire engine red fingernails.

"Ooooh, Fallah," Ms. Frizz cooed, with an orgasmic sigh, "That's much better."

Now this is America. What idiocy it has been for my people to worry about survival, about feeding hungry children, watching them go through all of childhood's little milestones, kissing them goodbye, and then sending them off to defend themselves against armies of crazed zealots. Or for Fallah to worry about her family, their fate unknown. There are much graver concerns here in this land of emancipation and opportunity. We have the freedom here to be able to choose, if we want, a life totally devoted to the worship of the self and to the adulation of the holy fingernail.

Chapter 6

REFRACTION

These (are) unsettling times,
when we are learning to recognize the truth,
by how deeply we long to disbelieve it.
— Francine Prose

For a few weeks' time, my feelings toward Danielle were kept tightly guarded, under lock and key. We met for regularly scheduled weekly supervisory sessions, where I tried to keep the discussions confined to professional issues. When Danielle made overtures toward less formal meetings, I tended to beg out, hiding behind the excuses of an overwhelming workload, and of my "mother guilt" to which she could well relate.

One Friday morning, when we were to have met for our weekly supervisory session, Danielle did not arrive on time. I ducked into the ladies' room, and there she was. She was standing over the sink, with red-rimmed eyes, she trembled uncontrollably. The color had been drained from her face, and she was gulping in air, much like a child after having had cried herself to sleep.

Instinctively, I put my arm around her.

"I'm sorry, Rach. I didn't want anyone to know. I am really blowing it, now."

"Tell me, Danielle," I said softly, "What's going on?"

"Oh, it's just so involved. I don't know where to begin. It's just that everything is falling to pieces." At this point, she started crying again, a fresh round of tears.

"Last month," she recounted, "Eric left for San Francisco. I knew he would. I knew he wanted to start up his practice all over again in a different area and make a fresh start. Well, two days ago, I came home after work, and found my house nearly empty. Apparently, he hired a moving van to pick up the furniture when I was away at work. I can't believe he would do this to his children." She resumed crying, again.

"And then, in yesterday's mail, I received an eviction notice."

"You mean you didn't own your brownstone?"

"Rented. It was part of the agreement that Eric would pay the rent for it. But he's just let it lapse."

"Do you think they would actually evict you for one month's rent?"

"Well," she continued between tears, "Eric moved out about a year ago. And it said on the notice that he stopped paying the rent six months ago — that our rent was six months overdue. I didn't know that. I had no idea."

"Can you call him?" I was holding my arms around her, now.

"He just split. I think he's flipped out. I don't know where to reach him, and neither does my attorney. Where do I write — 'Eric Schoenfeld, Number 1, San Francisco?' "

"Has he been giving you anything to live on?" (I knew what kind of salaries psych interns make).

"He was giving us something. Just barely something, a thousand dollars a month, up until last month. I've been checking the mail box every day, and it's just not there."

"Gosh." My arms were still around her. I felt myself instinctively rocking her, comforting her, as one would a child who just awoke from a nightmare. I felt somewhat foolish, uttering my monosyllabic idioms. Somehow no words would pop into my head which could give her adequate comfort, which could magically undo all the damage which her ex-husband had done to her. I suddenly found myself praying that these magic words of comfort would appear to me. Instead, I just asked, "How long has this been going on?"

"Well, all of a sudden it seems like the roaches are coming out of the woodwork. My landlord wants us out of there by the end of the month. He wants to repaint and sand down the floors, so that he can show it to some other renters," she said, between tears. "God. I don't know where we're going to live."

I just continued rocking her, holding her, like a colicky infant in my arms. "I feel so uprooted," she continued. "We're going to be homeless. I feel like a refugee in a displaced person's camp after the war! And I feel like Eric . . . like Eric's the Gestapo or something — out to get me."

Oh, please, God, I said to myself, *why THAT analogy? Why are you making my feelings so complicated, Danielle?* But I just continued rocking her, holding her, like she was my own little girl, and I would protect her from all the bad vultures and demons of the night.

"It's okay, Danielle," I said, almost instinctively. "Everything's gonna be all right. We have plenty of room at our house. . . . Really. There's no way in this world that you and the kids are ever going to be homeless."

She looked at me with gratitude. Her eyes were suddenly fragile and delicate. I really just wanted to make everything all right for her, at that moment. I really just wanted to make her crying stop, and to make everything all better for her, more than anything else in the world. I just wanted to tell her that this was all a bad dream. That in the morning, everything will be all right.

"Really?" she asked, incredulously.

"Really," I answered.

"You know, Rachel. I just don't know if I've got the stuff in me to survive. I've never been put to the test, before."

"Oh, come on, Danielle. You know you'll survive. You know it's just temporary."

"Well, I guess. If my father could survive all he had to go through, I can, too. I can survive anything. He did."

How can I adequately explain this tangled web of emotions that were running through my mind at that moment? Everything was so distorted, so twisted and confused. Here she was, again, referring to this saintly father. What was I to do? Take away her only comfort, her anchor, at what was probably to be the most distraught time of her life, when she was in more real distress than most people will ever know in a lifetime? I couldn't. I simply could not destroy her only idol. I could not tarnish his halo. Even though I knew deep down inside that he might have shoved my grandparents into the ovens.

All I knew was that at that moment I wanted to make everything all right for her. To rock her and comfort her in my arms. Was she becoming my Jewish victim? Was I her righteous Gentile? Was this, somehow, a fantasy of hers that she wanted to live out? Was her identification with the Jewish victim so strong? Had she subconsciously orchestrated all of this in her head, and was I playing along? Playing along with this perverted, delusional life script that was being mediated by a guilt-ridden subconscious? Was I falling right into it, saying all the right lines ? Was her Jewish husband becoming distorted, in this script, into a Nazi war criminal? Her father, with his dubious history, into a Raoul Wallenberg? Were the landlords suddenly transformed into the hundreds of thousands of "good Germans" who innocently, silently collaborated with the Nazis and turned in Jews? Was I not a collaborator in this delusion of hers by my silence, by my tacit refusal to utter what I knew, deeply laden within me, like the blood which flows through my veins, to be the truth about her father?

I didn't know . . . and, at that moment, I didn't care. All I knew, as I stood there, was that I wanted a bit of peace for her in her tumultuous life. All I knew was that I wanted her pain and throbbing and crying to stop.

"Please," I prayed to myself, silently, "Bubbie and Zadie in heaven that I never knew. Please forgive her. If there is a force in history, if there is some sort of moral score that's being settled by someone up there, please don't do this to her. It was just an accident of biology that she happened to be born to her parents, and that I happened to be born to mine. Please. Please. Don't let her suffer for the sins of her father."

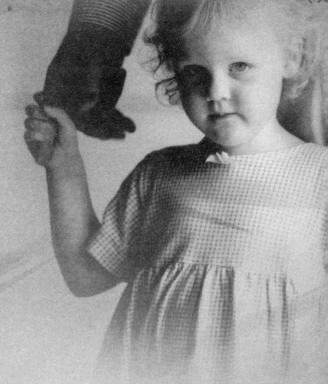

Chapter 7

STATIC FORCES

> We are all brothers, and we are all suffering the
> same fate. The same smoke floats over all our heads.
> Help one another. It is the only way to survive.
> — An "old" prisoner speaking to a new
> concentration camp arrival,
> as recorded in Elie Wiesel's *Night*

I arrived at the office early the next morning to find Danielle bent over her desk, scoring some test protocols. She looked up at me gratefully and smiled, a full radiant smile, as someone who has just seen the first rays of sunshine after a flood of terror only can.

"Good news, Rach. My attorney was able to track down Eric through the A.M.A. directory. She said she is going to be able to secure a temporary support order, now. We don't have to move, after all. At least not this second. She told me that Eric said the move had been really chaotic, and that now that he's settled, he'll be sending something in the mail, any day now."

"Do you believe him?"

"Not for one second, but at least he is aware that we know where he lives, and that he can't run and hide from us and just shirk any responsibility toward us. I mean they are his children, too!"

"What sort of clout does this give you, though? I mean what sort of teeth do you have to sink into him to actually make sure that you do get the check in the mail?"

"Well, I'm not really positive," she said tossing a stray blond strand off of her forehead, "but my attorney did mention that she's shooting to get a court date for the end of this month for the separation agreement, and lack of payment certainly doesn't help his case any."

"What if he pleads poverty?"

"He can't. We have our last few years' statements of earnings from the IRS. He'd have to be pretty extravagant to blow away a half a million a year."

"*What* — a half a million a year? Why did he leave you penniless — and almost homeless? He must have tremendous assets! How could a person like that pack up and take your furniture out of the house? He must be some kind of a schmuck." I felt the heat rising into my face, reddening my complexion.

"Yeah. A very special kind. At least he thinks so."

"What do you mean?"

"Well, I know that part of his income has gone, in the past, to pay off other ex-patients of his who he practiced his very special brand of medicine on."

"Oh, I can't stand it! You're kidding me!"

"No, it's true." Her face was flushed now. Her voice was quieter. I knew she was revealing something deeply distressing, perhaps deeply embarrassing to her. "Shortly after Eric and I married," she went on, "he mentioned something about a financial obligation to some lunatic ex-patient of his, just to keep her quiet. Like the dutiful wife that I was, I just didn't think about it. I didn't want to think about it, I guess."

"But then letters started coming to the house. There was more than one. The worst thing about it was that I later found out that some of these affairs were going on even after he married me. I thought I had swept him off his feet, and he was head over heels in love with me."

"Oh, God," I said, sharing in her agony, as only two women can, in that marvelous sisterhood of friendship which knows no ethnic bounds. "I am really beginning to hate this person."

"Not nearly as much as I," she stated, not without a good amount of passion in her voice. "Do you want to know the worst?" she continued, in a voice which hinted that she was about to emotionally disrobe, and reveal that under that beautiful English mohair sweater, which seems to wrap such an inviting form, was simply warts, molds, and tissue paper. "The worst," she continued, raising her eyebrows, "was that I felt unattractive, ugly, sexless. Why else would he do this to me? Why would he need so many women, if I were attractive enough to satisfy him?"

This, I could not let her believe. My leanings as an empiricist and an objective observer of the human species were far too strong. And she was far too gorgeous, both empirically and objectively, to walk around with such a delusion in her head. Some delusions were more easily arguable than others . . . and this one, I just could not allow her to harbor any longer.

"Danielle," I said, taking her hand in mine, "you cannot . . . you simply cannot believe this. Woman to woman, I have to tell you that you are truly beautiful — uncommonly beautiful. You really must know it." I said this with some manner of certitude. How could she not? Every time she walks down the street, all pairs of eyes, particularly of the male species, follow her.

"Really?"

"Yes. Really." I said this in an almost exasperated tone, as though I had just been trying to teach her to tie her shoelaces for the 25th time. "I mean it. As your supervisor, I have one final thing left to teach you" (I assumed a matronly voice) "and that is that you're beautiful . . . truly . . . rarely." We exchanged girlish giggles for a brief moment.

She looked at me with those child-like eyes again, as though I was spoon-feeding her some hope to hang onto.

"Thank you, Rachel," she said, taking my hand. "I was really beginning to doubt even that. And this one, this hurt even more than losing my Georgetown house, my status as a rich doctor's wife, my furniture. This one really hit home."

"Hey," I said, almost impulsively, "speaking of furniture . . . I have one final question for you. What is it that you're sleeping on?"

"Well, Eric didn't take the kids' beds. I've been sharing a bed with Leah, just for the time being."

"Is it okay if you let me do something for you?" I asked, impetuously. "Can we just go over to Cort Furniture Rental and get you some decent furniture? Just for the time being, till you get over this hump."

"That's very nice. But let me think about it." I thought for a moment, that she might have been overwhelmed by my generosity, but instead, she said, "I'd rather you and David co-sign on a loan for me. So that I could buy things. Of quality, I mean? You just don't know who has slept on a bed from Cort Furniture Rental. You know, with this crazy disease and stuff."

"Sure. If that's what you need. I'll ask David about it." Although I was almost certain that AIDS does not get transmitted by sharing a rental bed, but by what goes on on top of the rental bed, but if this is what she needed to survive, so be it. I did have a strong feeling that the idea of sleeping on furniture of inferior quality was what was actually bothering her. If she was to possess anything at all, even just temporarily, it had to have come from off the floor of Bloomingdale's, or not at all. Well, I figured, if this is what she needed to get by, why not?

"In the meantime, what do we do to celebrate your good news? I can make us reservations at Clyde's in Georgetown. Or maybe Flutes? Let's start the champagne pouring."

"I'll tell you what," she responded. "Instead of going out drinking with me, can you do me a bigger favor?"

"Sure . . . shoot."

"My kids, they're so confused. Eric was the real Jew in the house. They know I converted because of him. And there's their Jewish father running off to San Francisco. They need some consistency, some stability in their lives."

"What is it that you actually want from me, Danielle?" I was confused. And also a bit in awe of all her pre-arranged agendas. She seemed to be so much in control of the situation, and to know what she needed and wanted from each of the key players in her life. She really was a survivor. Much more so than I could be, under her circumstances, I thought.

"Well, what I really want," she cleared her throat, "is for the kids and myself to come over for Friday night dinner."

"Is that all? The way you built that up, I thought you were going to ask me if I could lend you David for a few years, to be a father to them." We again exchanged laughter, the way only two girlfriends can.

"No. It's just really important to me. In a way that you can't realize — that you probably never will. You could be my Jewish connection — a kind of spiritual anchor for me. I'm just so afraid I'm going to lose my connection to Judaism now that Eric's out of the picture. And if there's one thing I know I've wanted my entire life it is to be a Jew. I know that I was meant to be one — it's my very essence. And the kids, they're so confused. I think they're beginning to hate Eric, which is all right, I guess, under the circumstances, but I just don't want them to hate all men, or all Jews. You know, I converted after we were married a few years."

"No. I didn't realize.."

"Yeah, they still remember it. Max thought the *mikvah* was a swimming pool. The rabbis were about to disrobe and jump in to rescue him!"

"I guess you don't forget an experience like that!" We exchanged laughter, again.

"Sure, Danielle. You can come over every Friday night if you want. That's no problem. We do the whole thing up, every week, anyway. We'll just add a little more water to the chicken soup." We were in a girlish, giggly mood, and ended the conversation with plans for dinner that Friday night, and more laughter.

It was set then. Danielle and her children were to arrive at our house that Friday night for dinner. In the meantime, loan papers from the Hebrew Free Loan Society arrived in our mail box. *Ironic*, I thought to myself, as David and I lent our signatures to the bottom of the page, *this loan company was established in the 1930s by a group of prominent German Jewish benefactors to help some of their fellow expatriates on the run from Hitler to re-establish their lives in this country.*

And what of the mansion in Princeton — that picture on the mantle of her fireplace, of her girlhood home? What happened to all the assets from that estate? I know that her father is dead, but where are his assets, and where is her mother, now? Why isn't she there to help her daughter, in this, her time of need?

I must admit I was more than a littler bit nervous about Danielle's presence in our house for dinner. It wasn't simply her upper-class polish and Princeton patina. It was more than that. It had more to do with my insatiable curiosity about this creature, and about who her family was, and what he and his kind might have done to me and my kind. Try as I might, to feel for

Danielle and her plight, on a personal level I simply could not exorcise these lingering thoughts from the back of my brain, where they were constantly gnawing away at me. I did not like the feel of this confusing interplay of emotions. Was I betraying my father's memory by helping this person? But here she was, just barely treading water to get by. How could I not throw her a raft?

But deep down inside, knowing my father the way I did, I somehow had the feeling he would have done the same thing, given the chance. He would have had the insight to see past the Bavarian wrapping paper of her little ontological package, and just recognize another person in need. Almost instinctively, I knew my father would have opened his heart to this poor, confused person whose life seemed to have overnight been suspended into the sheer terror of limbo, a terror he had known so well. After all, she had no more say in the matter of whose womb she was born out of than I did. That was a mere accident of biology. We are what we make ourselves to be, not what has been determined for us by some random free-floating DNA molecule at the moment of conception. What mattered is that she needed a raft immediately, and I was prepared to throw her one. My father would not have done any differently. I was certain of that.

That night, I drifted to sleep, exhausted, with my children, still clothed in my work clothes. I dreamt that I called Danielle and said I couldn't make it into the office because Benyamen was sick, running a slight fever. "Oh, that's easy enough," Danielle responded, in my dream. "My brother's over now. He's a pediatrician, and he's great with children. Just drop Benyamen off here, and we'll leave for the schools to do some testing from here."

The scene shifted in my dream to a pristine garden in Princeton, replete with climbing red rose bushes adorning white trellises and green wrought iron garden furniture. Danielle's brother emerged. A strikingly handsome man with sandy blond hair, a golden tan, and a strong chin, in a brown shirt. For some reason, I was reluctant to hand Benyamen over to him. He kept stroking his hair, and asking him if he had to use the bathroom. Why was he doing that, I asked myself, in my sleep. Were there showers or ovens in the bathroom? What sort of experiments was this good doctor going to perform on my beautiful first-born son?

Benyamen ran off to play among the trellises and rose bushes. And I was scared. I was scared I was going to lose my child forever — lost to some maniac's master plan.

I awoke in terror, still in bed with each of my two sons sleeping peacefully at my side. I held each of them closely to my breast, and kissed them with wet, silent kisses, grateful — hardly believing that this dream of having my children next to me, their chests rising and falling rhythmically, without having their sleep interrupted by some madman's utopian design, is the reality that I now occupy. Knowing that I could not have survived, I do not have the stuff it takes, to survive that other nightmarish reality when children were routinely ripped from their mother's breasts in the name of some greater good for humankind. I also knew that among the greatest gifts our fragile, finite little lives have to enjoy is that of watching the gentle, uninterrupted slumber of children.

Yes, I resolved to myself. I could be Danielle's righteous Gentile for her. I would throw her a raft, or whatever it took for her to survive, and for her children to sleep in uninterrupted slumber. What I was determined to do, however, was to find out some details about her father's life, some basic facts about him. To, at the very least, get her maiden name, his name, as a start. Just to put an end to this gnawing, throbbing ache at the back of my head and to these terrifying dreams.

Chapter 8

PRISMS OF LIGHT

Our house. . . . Is a very, very, very fine house with
two cats in the yard, Life used to be so hard,
Now everything is easy cause of you.
— Crosby, Stills, Nash, and Young

Behold how good and how pleasant it is for
brothers and sisters to dwell together in unity.
— The Book of Psalms

My heart was pounding heavily when the doorbell rang. In
marched Danielle and her little troupe, one more beautiful than
the next. Introductions and apologies were quickly exchanged,
because they drove up to the house way past sunset. The children seemed to drift into the room, carrying with them the
fresh vapors of Georgetown Prep. Nicole, age 15, was definitely
the most exotic of the little clan. Her thick ashen brown hair
draped gracefully around her finely sculpted face, adorned with

dimples and a smattering of freckles over her perfectly cast nose. She was wearing a very clingy black jersey knit, and was obviously aware that she had what it takes to fill it up quite nicely. She had a manner of brushing that thick mane of hair out of her eyes with a sensuous upward flick of her head, that only a 15 year old with that new, hot, emerging sense of herself as a sexual being knows how to do. Max, age 12, seemed to have spent his formative nursery years on the Congressional Country Club tennis courts. He seemed forever comfortable in his Banana Republic shirt with the label turned outward, and his well-fitted Jordache jeans, which seemed to be worn out in precisely the right places. He carried with him that easy, casual sense of humor and grace of presence that could only have been transmitted from the maternal side. And Leah, age 6, with her buoyant, radiant smile, her deep auburn hair, and her infectious laugh immediately stole all of our hearts away.

The first of our little troupe to express enthusiasm over their presence was McDavid, our shaggy, ungroomed bearded collie, who attacked them with licks and yelps. The name, a natural conversation starter, immediately stole their curiosity.

"Well the breed is Scottish, and when he was whelped the breeders named him McDuffy. When we got him, we decided to Hebraize it and name him McDavid . . . McDovey, for short."

"Oh, mom," Nicole droned, "McDovey . . . I love it. . . . A Jewish dog."

At this point, David (forever the proud parent) decided to step in and show off a bit of his mastery as a dog trainer. "McDovey," he commanded, "here boy." We all followed their lead into the kitchen where David filled his empty dog bowl. McDovey bent over it, intent on eating, when David interrupted with "Traif." Immediately, McDovey held back, waiting till he heard the promised word, "Kosher," at which he instantly devoured his meal.

"I can't stand it. It's incredible," Nicole enthused, "He's Jewish *and* kosher."

I beamed to myself, the self-satisfied smile of a proud Jewish mother, forever conscious somewhere in the back of my head of their lineage and mine, and wondering whether or not this wasn't a minor sort of posthumous victory for mine. I had an immediate, intensely gratifying vision of a Nazi storm trooper turning over loudly in his grave.

The children were truly beautiful. I marveled at how easily mine mingled with Danielle's. Max brandished a deck of cards, and began to amuse my two delighted sons Benyamen, age 8, and Joshua, age 5, with his artfully developed skill as a magician. I realized very quickly that their eyes were developing that special glow of glee in them reserved only for mythical heroes and young teenage idols. Joshua climbed onto his lap and began pleading, "Show me how you did that one, Max!" Max moved his index finger as if to say, "I'll let you in on a little secret," and motioned him downstairs, into the basement. Joshua soon ascended up the basement steps, from then on, eagerly trying out his newly learned trick on everyone, throughout the evening.

I was left in awe of Danielle and her little troupe, all so polite, so calm, so composed, under these very trying and stressful circumstances. How could they appear to be so anchored when their lives were undergoing such turmoil? They gave the impression that they were at the helm of their lives, that they had everything under perfect control, when, in actuality, the floor was being torn out from under them. Had Danielle managed to so effectively shield them from the apparent chaos of their lives, or was this simply a well-cultivated veneer, a new breed of adolescent coolness and sophistication, or perhaps their coping skills were so great that they managed to swim over these rocky waters with ease. If so, we should trade places, I thought to myself, *You kids sit at my desk. I'll lie on the couch.*

Danielle entered the kitchen with me, to help me serve. I had decided to make a very traditional Jewish dinner. Danielle went into rhapsodies when she learned that the first course would be chicken soup with matzah balls. "Oh, I'm so glad you made this," she exclaimed. "It's my favorite. It really isn't Friday evening without this. *(My goodness*, I thought to myself, *such rapture over a matzah ball?)* Reification. Luckas didn't realize how prescient he was. She bent her head over the huge soup pot, and began dishing the soup with a large wooden ladle into the blue and white delft china bowls. She looked at me warmly, gratefully, tiny beads of sweat from the steam of the chicken soup forming on her forehead, and uttered, "You really can't imagine what this means to me and my family. Someday I'll tell you. It has to do with my family . . . it's . . . oh, never mind."

The evening went so well, better than my greatest expectations. Joshua and Leah seemed to have found the keys to one another's heart by speaking their own private 5 and 6-year-old language (making rhymes of the more adult conversation, intermingled with hearty giggles every few moments). It was one of those meals that I had put my heart into preparing, from the chicken soup to the chocolate decadence cake with the raspberry chocolate topping.

The conversation was mostly centered around the children and the various types of miserable, stodgy old teachers we had all had in our pasts. We took turns mimicking some of our "favorites," and their particular idiosyncrasies. "My French teacher, Madam Pompadour, Je m'appelle Madam Pooompadooore," Nicole said, as we all burst out into full-bodied laughter. "No budy spiks Anglis in Madame Pooompadooore's classrum," she said, dramatically above our laughter, obviously enjoying her audience as much as we enjoyed her little act.

The Sabbath candles on the dining room table were dwindling. We retired to the living room, well fed and relaxed, and sat comfortably on the sofa and easy chairs. "Speaking of

French," David said, casually, "How did you decide on Nicole's name? It is French, isn't it"

"Right after I gave birth," Danielle said, "while I was still in the hospital, I had this dream. I dreamt I was in the French Riviera, and there was a gorgeous girl in a white sailor dress with flowing brown hair. She was wearing a cute little white sailor's cap. I was calling out to her, "Nicole, Nicole." And when I woke up, I knew that would be my daughter's name. And the uncanny thing is how much Nicole looks like that girl in my dream. (Nicole smiled coyly, batting her mascared eyelashes, dramatically.)

"And Max?" David asked, "how did you hit upon his name?"

"Oh, the moment he was born and let out that gutsy scream, I knew he was a Max. So savvy. Even as a baby. He just always had this earthy air of intelligence about him — a kind of *savoir faire*. I hit the nail on the head with him. My Max with all his maxi."

"And Leah?" he asked, taking natural command of the conversation.

"Well she was born after we had already converted to Judaism. She was going to be my little Jewish princess. I thought that was the absolute best name for a Jewish baby."

"Yeah," Max quickly interjected," Leah Schoenfeld. I can just picture her in some poor apartment in Brooklyn, with a *babooshka* over her head, baking challahs." (We were hysterical).

"And your kids?" Danielle asked.

"Well, you know Benyamen was named after Rachel's father, who died a few months before he was born. And Joshua — we just always loved that name, Joshua. We knew if we ever had another son, it would be a Joshua," David said.

"It is a beautiful name. They both are," Danielle offered.

"Well, it seems to have really come into vogue as of late," I said. "Every time I'm at an upscale shopping center with lots of yuppies and their little yuppie puppies, I hear, "Joshua, where are you?"

"Yes, I hear a lot of biblical names of late. Joshua, Aaron, Sarah, Rebecca, Noah, Adam," Danielle recited, twirling a strand of her flaxen hair with a finger.

"It's true," David said. "There seem to be definite trends in what people choose to name their children. A few years ago it was Jennifer, Jessica, Kimberly, Justin, Seth, Kevin."

"Before that," said Danielle, "it was cute stuff like Candy, Sandy, Suzie."

"Yuck," said Max, deadpan, "I'm getting sick from all this sweetness."

"But our parents' generation was just the opposite," said David. "Their parents picked names that were distinguished sounding, kind of pretentious — like Oscar, Herman, Reuben. My father's name, for example, was Maurice."

How brilliant, I thought. *Where is David leading this conversation? Could it possibly be that he's maneuvering it to uncover Danielle's father's name?* Oh, how much lust and libido I suddenly felt for this keen-witted man I was wedded to.

"And my father's name was Wilhelm — Wilhelm Von Hoffmann, later Anglicized to William Hoffman," said Danielle.

"Boy, Leah Schoenfeld has sure come a long way from Wilhelm Von Hoffmann," said Max.

We all laughed, that kind of easy, effortless laugh of friends who have shared a lovely evening together. I, of course, laughing, in private, a little bit more heartily, that the tides of history had proven not to eliminate the Sarahs and Rebeccas and Rachels and Leahs, but the Gustavs and the Franzs and the Wilhelms and the Hanzes. (Another posthumous victory for my father and his people.)

They left, exchanging goodbye's, thank-you's, kisses, hugs, full of genuine *bonhomie.*

I gently closed the mahogany door behind them, and lingered there a moment, filled with a mixture of affection and admiration for Danielle and her little family, and resolved to do whatever I could to help them, whatever it would take, while all the while, in the back of my mind, I was reciting Wilhelm Von Hoffmann, alias William Hoffman, her dead father's name, silently to myself, over and over again, until it was etched indelibly in my brain.

Chapter 9

SHATTERED
FRAGMENTS

We may, with advantage, at times,
forget what we know.
— Publilius Syrus, *Maxims*

Danielle called at the very moment the Sabbath was over. I imagined that she had been standing out in the cold evening air, waiting for three stars to emerge which symbolically marks the close of the Sabbath — her timing was that precise. Her voice was buoyant with light and energy. "Thank you so much for dinner last night. You have no idea how meaningful it was for me and the kids. Your family is like a little spiritual nest for us in an insane world of vultures."

"Danielle, listen. It's so little for me. Please. I don't deserve any thanks. Any time you want. You and the kids could be regular guests at our table on Friday night. We always manage to do it up right, anyway, somehow." (This, by the way, was very true. Whatever the chaos of our weekly lives may bring, Friday night dinner is invariably set aside as special, and manages, sometimes rather miraculously, to get on the table before sunset).

"Oh, that's such a comforting thought. It's just so nice that you're there for me, Rach, at this particular time in my life. I'm so glad I happened to stumble upon you, and that you're there for me, with your Judaism and all."

"I am. And I will be. Whatever happens."

"Thank you, friend. Might I call you that?"

"Absolutely. Might I call you that?" We laughed together, the sweet, light laughter of women friends, and hung up the phone bidding adieu until Monday.

Monday morning. I walked through the 1950s school-style, white brick corridors of my office with a new lilt and urgency in my steps. I seemed to have gotten a booster shot of adrenaline from this newly germinating friendship. I had recently begun to realize how precious this relationship was to me, just how much I had missed the sweet friendship of a woman. As though I had just discovered a barren place in my anatomy which had existed for a long time, like a woman who accidentally conceives, finding this love for her unborn child within herself, and wondering how she could have lived so many years without fulfilling that side of her. Yes, it's been a long time since I laughed easily with another woman friend, in only the way that two women can. Perhaps since Rivka's departure to Israel. . . . I was anxious to see Danielle, and renewed my resolve to myself to do whatever I could to help her, whatever it took.

I suddenly had to use the bathroom. I quickly ducked into the ladies' room. Behind the closed door of the Lysol-scented toilet stall, I could hear Danielle's voice, mingled with that of my supervisor. They had entered the bathroom. I could see the glossy black patent-leather shoes with golden buckles of my supervisor, and Danielle's well-worn, beige Papagello's from under the door of the bathroom stall. I heard them talking freely, oblivious to anyone else's presence.

"You know, Rachel is really getting burned out."

"I know, her productivity has really gone downhill these last few months."

"I know. She's been talking to me about easing up on her hours to spend more time at home with the boys. After I finish my year of supervision, I will be certified and employable, if you do have any vacancies available. In case Rachel does decide to quit or something. She really should, you know. Maybe you could encourage her to. Her heart's really not in this, anymore. I just wanted to let you know I'm available for September."

I could feel the blood quickly draining from my face. A complete sense of betrayal quickly overcame me. Who was this person I was supervising, anyway, that one minute ago I felt this indivisible bond of friendship toward. And, more importantly, what made her tick? It was true, perhaps, that I was getting tired, burned out, as I had confided to Danielle — but was that for her to reveal to my supervisor? Who was this person who just an instant ago I was full of love for, and resolve to help, in any way?

I debated with myself. Should I flush and emerge from the toilet stall and let her know I had overheard the entire conversation? Or should I play-act in an innocent charade that I hadn't heard a word, and wait out this long conversation, in hiding here, in this bathroom stall, until the sound of their footsteps has long disappeared down the corridor? The smell of the Lysol was beginning to get to me. I was feeling slightly nauseous, queasy. I don't know if it was the smell of the Lysol, or the inner knowledge that I could never successfully carry off that charade of innocence. That I never could manage to successfully handle duplicity. In a rare act of courage, or rather, impulse, I decided to flush, and emerged from the toilet stall.

Danielle and my supervisor saw me, exchanged nervous glances, and left the ladies' room in silence.

We walked back to the office together, in an awkward, heavy, silence. Finally, behind the closed, oak door of my office, Danielle flashed me a bitter, disgusted look. Her azure eyes, now seemed more of a Prussian blue. She turned to me, with more of an aura of moral righteousness and certitude than of apology, and said, "You don't understand, Rachel. You wouldn't. But I can never forget. My father hardly made a living during the war. He was brilliant. He was trained as a physicist and an engineer, but refused to use it to help the Nazis. He came here without any papers. Do you realize what it means for a person like that to have to work as a plumber? To have to unclog people's stuffed-up toilet bowls?"

I had very little sympathy for her at this point. Even if this story was true, which I doubted greatly, this did not compare with what my parents had been through during the war years. In my characteristic silence, I let her continue on.

"And the Nazis, in their vindictiveness, refused to forward his papers. They refused to release them, so that he couldn't get a decent job in this country. Berlin was bombed, and his papers. He had to work after the war as a mechanical engineer, a much more lowly job than he could've gotten had he remained in Germany, without any benefits or security. That taught me a very valuable lesson — that I would do whatever I had to do to survive. That I would never be stripped of my honor and dignity, like my father was."

Oh, God, I thought to myself, trying to swallow that all-too-familiar taste of bile. All the lacunae of her fairy tale story about her father are beginning to come together at once. Why would the Nazis bomb Berlin, anyway, their own city? Could it be that he came here without papers, not because the Nazis felt he was betraying them, but because he didn't want to disclose what sorts of activities he had actually been involved in during the war years? *And what does that mean*, I continued thinking. *I would do whatever I had to do to survive.* Does this mean she would've complied with the Nazis for her own survival? Go to the Gestapo to inform on a Jewish friend, in hiding, somewhere? Is that not unlike what she's doing now? Informing on me? Betraying on my confidence, my friendship?

In a sudden, rare act of courage, I said, in a soft, tired voice, "It's really ironic. My father was also stripped of his dignity during the war." The hue of her face suddenly deepened to a dark crimson.

". . . And my father also came here without his professional papers. I might venture to add that he lost a lot more than his professional papers during the war. That was, you know, the very least of it." Now my complexion was dark crimson, I could feel the hotness, the wetness of it. "But before the war he had received his master's degree in German philosophy and literature from the University of Heidelberg, you know. But refused to use it, after the war."

"Why?" She looked at me witlessly, incongruously. "Because there wasn't a demand for that after the war?"

"No," I said in a barely audible, fatigued voice, like that of a teacher weary of having to repeat a basic lesson from a reading primer. "No, because that was the language that had been used to mangle his life and to murder his family."

She looked down as though examining the tiny cracks between the boards of the pine floor. I could almost feel her perspiration, could hear her heavy breathing. She did not want to hear this. I knew that. The facts of my father's life and my people's suffering were like vexing little thorns in the back, aggravating little details in the background of the real drama of her father's suffering, a suffering so great that it would justify whatever it took, not to put herself in the same circumstances in her own lifetime. That was the moral of this little fairy tale of hers: I will not be like my heroic father who sacrificed his career for his principles. I will do whatever it takes to survive.

She did not want to look at my face, I knew. She quickly excused herself and left the room.

Oh, Danielle, the tangled, enmeshed interplay of emotions you evoke within me. I was confused, perplexed. Compassion for her was intermingled with sharp feelings of disgust and betrayal, like the rose in a paint box, mixing with bilious green, and becoming a muddy brown. Nothing was clear to me. Nothing was pure anymore, without ambiguity. What did Danielle know about her father? Were any of these blatant lacunae of her story about him clear to her? They were so obvious to me. How could such an intelligent, articulate girl as Danielle not be aware that the war was over in 1945 — the date she told me he came to these shores? Why would the Nazis bomb Berlin? Where did he get the money for that mansion in Princeton?

Were these the fairy tales that he had gently rocked her to sleep with, so that he, too, could watch the sweet uninterrupted slumber of his child, at night? No harm done. Let her believe whatever is more pleasant for the child, so that the loving glow of adoration of this beautiful, blond little girl for her daddy never leaves her eyes?

Or was this a fairy tale of her own invention? Designed hastily from little pieces and snatches of facts, quickly fastened together with the delusive scotch tape of a little girl's desire to keep worshiping her adoring father? He looked so handsome under this rosy, heroic hue. Why spoil the picture with some ugly brown details from the Third Reich, even if the scotch tape is beginning to lose some of its viscidity?

At what point is an illusion a delusion? Is it a matter of conscious volition of belief, of some sort of self-awareness? Was this a conscious act of will, of her own invention, or was it something that had been spoon fed to her since birth, that she simply chose not to question, but swallowed whole, in perfect faith, like a tale from the Book of Genesis?

What was making her do this? Was it fear? Hunger? Had she received a check from Eric in the mail, yet? There she was, just at my house this past Friday night, and she must have noticed how solid my relationship is with David. Maybe she knows I'll always have him there to depend on, while she will be out there on the streets, struggling to support her family, on her own. But where is her trust, there? Does the fear of hunger create such desperate behavior? Perhaps it does. She may well feel that she's being confronted with the problem of survival, here, for herself and her family. Desperate situations sometimes make for desperate solutions. I had once said that before.

I left the office, in an interminable state of confusion.

Perhaps I had been wrong about her, all along, I thought. Sorely wrong. The words of Winston Churchill began to ring through my mind. "What a strange thing heredity is. We are all really only variants of what has gone before." Here I was, ready to open up my heart and my home to her, and all along, in her eyes, I had been just another disposable Yid.

Chapter 10

Dissolution

You know — my flower. I am responsible for her.
And she is so weak! She is so naive!
She has four thorns, of no use at all,
to protect herself against the world.
— Antoine de Saint Exupery, *The Little Prince*

I have often been confounded by the amazing relationship between the mind and the body. The mind's sphere of influence pervades everywhere. From one's sense of self-esteem and how one presents himself in dress and demeanor, on the macroscopic level, to the relationship between one's effect and the body's immune system, or how vigorously our white blood cells mobilize themselves against foreign viruses or invading diseases, on the microscopic level. In no case, have I found this to be quite so apparent, as in the case of Danielle Schoenfeld.

As these real-life hardships in Danielle's life began to occur, her appearance began to gradually change. At times, I thought to myself, she barely resembled that ravishing blond who first entered my office, which now seemed an eternity ago. A worn, tired look was constantly etched across her face. Her eyes, once so clear, were now heavily bloodshot, and deeply hidden under dark shadows. Her face took on a constant drained, haggard quality. I worried that she wasn't eating. Her body, which once filled out her clothes so abundantly, now seemed drawn and emaciated. And her clothes now seemed to have lost that Princetonian patina. She always looked disheveled and unkempt, with rumpled clothes hastily and slovenly thrown across her body in a careless, random fashion.

My feelings about her were now suspended, bracketed, in a constant state of moral ambiguity. I could not help but pity this person whose life seemed to be going from riches to rags, corroding in front of my very eyes. Something inside of me, maybe this deeply rooted Jewish mother instinct, engraved permanently in my collective consciousness, made me want to forgive her for all of her inequities, despite myself. What did I have to worry about, anyway? I had tenure with the local school system. Despite Danielle's desperate attempts to lobby for my job, it was secure. I was just that — secure — walking on firm foundations in regard to just about everything in my life: my career, my relationship with my husband, my feelings toward my children, and in the clear unambiguous memory of what my mother and father had been for me. Danielle, on the other hand, was delicately tiptoeing along very shaky foundations. I didn't envy her at all.

Was I being too Christian-like, betraying myself by "turning the other cheek"? After all, we are the people who have been admonished to "Remember Amalek." No, the Judaism as I knew it, as I remember it as being exemplified by my father, my paradigm of morality, was a religion of compassion, if nothing else. I remember my father, his own body slowly ravaged with cancer, hardly being able to walk himself, painstakingly making his way down the halls of White Plains Hospital, dragging his "bad" leg slowly, painfully, one step at a time, behind his healthy one, visiting the "sick" every Friday before the Sabbath. I remember how the black janitor in our synagogue held his head in his chapped, work-worn hands, while I was in mourning for my father, and sobbed relentlessly, like a baby. "Cantor, cantor," he wailed between tears, "you were the only person who made me feel like a person."

And I remember how excited he was about the civil rights movement, sequestering off a precious dollar here or there to secretly send off to the NAACP. When asked why, he stated, simply and without eloquence, "Because every human being needs dignity" And when the civil rights marches and sit-ins began, in desperation, to disperse gradually into riots and lootings, I remember his very real sense of despair. But his only comment at that time was a quote from his beloved *Pirkei Avot*, The Teachings of the Fathers, *"Al Tadin Et Chavercha Ad Shetagiyah Bimkomo."* (Do not judge your friend, your fellow man, until you have been in his place.) No, the God of the Jewish people, whom we have been taught to emulate, is a God of compassion. He is described over and over again in the sacred texts and liturgy as being "gracious and full of mercy, slow to anger and abundant in loving kindness, and relenting of the evil decree."

No, I was not betraying my people by feeling compassion for this desperate person who was left with her very uncertain legacy. While I had the foundation of centuries to predicate my behavior upon, she was trying to scotch tape fantasy with illusion in her feeble attempt to piece together a heroic figure, a role model of morality, upon which to predicate hers. Oh, Danielle, how well I know that longing for him, and when he is gone, all that remains, in truth, is his example of how he carried out his life, the Teachings of the Fathers. *Pirkei Avot.*

When Danielle and I passed each other in the hall of the office the next day, she was visibly uncomfortable in my presence. I

was determined to act as normal and casual as possible. I vowed
to myself to never again mention that clandestine conference
in the ladies' room. I was determined to keep the conversation light, casual, professional. I brought up one of her cases,
Steven Williams, a seven-year-old black boy from Green Acres
Elementary School who was failing to learn to read, and had
become the object of ridicule of his classmates. Up until now
his behavior had been exemplary. But recently his behavior had
begun to deteriorate rapidly, becoming hostile and aggressive.
He had begun calling out names in class, picking fights on the
playground, tripping children on the way to their desks. Not an
unusual story.

"It's really a shame that children have to call attention to
themselves like that in order to get their basic needs met," I
said.

"Yeah," Danielle answered, "the squeaky wheel gets the most
oil. When he was quiet, nobody noticed his reading problem.
But now that he's beating up kids on the playground, everyone's
scheduled to service him. He's being seen by the reading teacher
next Monday, the educational diagnostician on Tuesday, the
speech pathologist on Wednesday, the school counselor on
Thursday, and I'm supposed to evaluate him on Friday."

"Poor kid," I said.

"Yeah, he really was calling out for help."

"Yeah. There's only so much humiliation a kid can take
before he starts acting out."

Although I resolved to ignore Danielle's bizarre bathroom
conference on Monday, and dismiss it as the desperate behavior
of a desperate person, I still could not exorcise that gnawing,
all-consuming curiosity about who her father was from my
brain. I decided I would finally do something about it. I was
determined to become a posthumous hunter of a particular
Nazi, if for nothing else, at least to put these constant, gnawing
questions in the back of my mind to rest.

Where to begin? I remember getting solicitations in the mail from the Simon Wiesenthal Center in Los Angeles. Well, it's a start.

I got home from the office early that evening, and quickly rummaged through the messy piles of unanswered mail on my desk. Ah, finally I came across an envelope from the Simon Wiesenthal Center with a letter inside, asking for contributions. (We were on the hit-list of every possible charity.) I quickly scanned the letter to the top of the page to the letterhead. There in black and white was a phone number, right under the address.

With trembling fingers, I quickly dialed the phone number.

The phone was ringing.

An interminable wait.

"Simon Wiesenthal Center. May I help you?"

"Yes. This is Rachel Stein. I'm calling from Maryland. I wonder if you might have a file on someone who I suspect might have been a Nazi."

"What was his name?" the pleasant but clipped voice on the other end of the line asked.

"Wilhelm Von Hoffmann. Later Anglicized to William Hoffman. He dropped the second 'n' in 'Hoffman' when he got to the States."

"Does he live in this country?" the anonymous voice on the other end of the line asked.

"Yes. Well, that is, he did. He died in 1980."

"Where was he from?"

"Germany, Berlin, actually."

"Do you know what he did during the war?"

"Not really. That's what I'd like to find out. His daughter said he did nothing. That's how I know about him — through his daughter. I know he was trained as a physicist and engineer. But she said he did nothing to hurt the Jews."

"What year did he get here?"

"1945."

"Hold on one moment. I'll see what we have on our computers."

Another endless wait.

"I'm sorry. Nothing is showing up under that name. You might try sending us that information in writing, and one of our researchers can investigate the case for you. And you might try writing to the Yad VaShem Archives in Jerusalem."

I thanked her, and hung up the phone.

That night, after I had tucked Benyamen and Joshua safely into their beds, I snuck off to my desk and quickly dashed off two letters, one destined toward Los Angeles and the other toward Jerusalem, carefully delineating all the information I knew concerning a certain Wilhelm Von Hoffmann, alias William Hoffman.

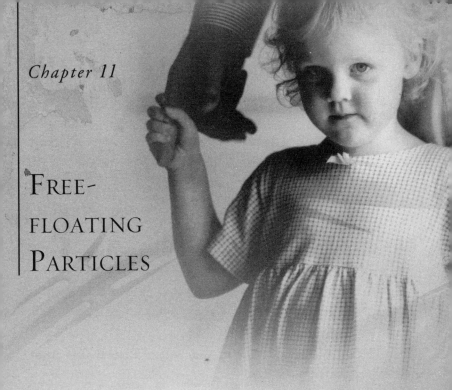

Chapter 11

FREE-FLOATING PARTICLES

Patrick, do not have revenge in your heart.
Only love and justice.
— Leo Baeck, in conversation with
U.S. Army Major Patrick Dolan, upon his
release from the Concentration Camp Theresienstadt

It had been weeks since I had sent off my letters to Los Angeles and Jerusalem. I hadn't yet heard from them, and was beginning to lose hope that I'd ever get any response. Every day, as soon as I returned from work, I anxiously checked the black metal mail box. No word.

In the meantime, Danielle's face was getting increasingly gaunter. Her eyes, almost hollow. Her body, skinny beyond the point of being attractive. I was worried that she might be anorexic or something.

Finally, one morning when she was looking particularly peaked, I asked her. "Danielle, you've been losing a lot of weight, lately. Have you been eating?"

"Just barely."

"What's been going on, Danielle?" I asked as nonchalantly as I could. "Is it money?"

"Frankly, yes."

"Has Eric sent any of the payments?"

"Nope. It's been months since we've received anything in the mail. The children and I are trying to live off of my income. We've eliminated everything from our lives but the bare essentials. And frankly, pretty soon, if things don't let up, I don't even think there's gonna be money for that."

"Hadn't your lawyer secured some sort of a temporary support order?" I asked.

"Yes. But Eric has simply chosen to ignore it. And apparently, he's managed to get away with it — at least up until now. It's not exactly legal, but if you cross state lines, it's much harder for them to catch up with you. We now have to open up a file in California. It might take years. It seems as though what happens in a courthouse in Maryland has very little impact on what's going on in California. Out of state cases just fall into little boxes and little black holes, and end up gathering dust on someone's desk.

"That's incredible. There must be a lot of women in your position, then."

"There are. And a lot of them are now in shelters for the homeless, or out in the streets. I've actually contacted the National Organization for Women, and they told me that they are aware of thousands of women in my situation across the country. Some attorneys actually advise their male clients to just cross interstate lines, to avoid making alimony and child support payments. Anyway, NOW basically told me that there's very little that they could do, at this point in time, because of the intricacies of interstate laws, unless some legislation is enacted on a federal level to hold people responsible for alimony and child support once they cross state lines."

"Are they trying to make that come about?"

"Yeah. They even recommended that I write my congresswoman about it, which I already have. I received a semi-personal letter from her, saying she's aware that there's an inequity in the system, and that she's working to enact some sort of a change on the national level in the U.S. Congress. But changes in legislation come about very slowly. In the meantime, we might be out on the streets, or starve, or both."

"Have you been able to make the rent payments?"

"Actually, my landlord has just about had it with me, and with listening to my excuses. He put another eviction notice in my box yesterday. He says he doesn't want to do this, but he has no choice. He actually said that if he wants to give to charity, there are others on his list he would prefer to give to."

"How disgusting." Then, reflexively, immediately, without thinking, I added, "Listen, Danielle. You know you'll never be out on the streets. You and the kids are always welcome to live with us. David and I have plenty of room in the house."

"I am down to going through old coats looking for loose change. I never thought for a moment that things would come to this. My lawyer is trying to arrange for a hearing in a few weeks. He wants to prove that Eric has been acting in contempt of court by not making any of the alimony or child support payments. Then we have to find an attorney in California to open up the case in the California courts. It's called a URESA case.

"But the way Eric is acting. . . . He's like a desperate man. He's mad. It's like the madness of Hitler when he knew that he was faced with defeat in the last few weeks of the war, speeding up the gassings in the concentration camps, even though he knew it wouldn't help him win the war on the front lines."

Why, Danielle, why must you always bring up that metaphor? Can't we ever have one single conversation where you don't make reference to the war or to the Holocaust? Can't you see that I'm trying to look at you as a person? An individual, in need of help? But whenever you bring it up, you distort reality in this perverted and nauseating way and claim the suffering of my people as your own. You and I both know intuitively whose father was the victim and whose the murderer. Some things people know intuitively. Not everything is so relative and perverted! But just as intuitively, I knew that the only thing I could do is offer this person a haven in my house. It was, really, the only thing to do.

"I'm serious, Danielle," I said. "I can't just watch you fade away like this in front of my eyes. I thought you were becoming anorexic! You're welcome to stay with us for as long as it takes for you and the kids to get back on your feet."

Long pause, then Danielle said softly, wearily, like a fatigued soldier after a long battle, "I think we just might have to take you up on it, this time. My landlord is really serious about evicting us, now. He wants to come in to the house next week to paint, sand down, and rewax the floors to be able to show it to a new tenant. He's asked that I put my remaining stuff into storage until I can move. I'm not really sure what other options I have left, right now. You have no idea of the terror and anguish I'm feeling right now." She looked at me. "You're sure you mean it, Rach?"

"Sure, I'm sure."

As Danielle left the office, I shook her hand, pressing a crisp one hundred dollar bill into her palm, as I was doing it.

"Thanks, friend," she said to me, gratefully. "I may call you that again, mightn't I?"

"Of course you may, friend." We hugged each other, a long hug like that of old friends meeting at a train station after a long interval of separation, perhaps six long forgotten years, and she quickly left the room.

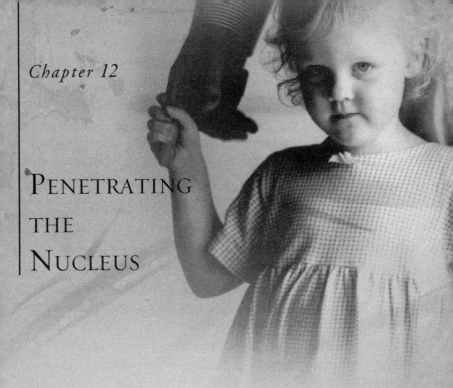

Chapter 12

Penetrating the Nucleus

Each thing, insofar as it is in itself,
endeavors to presevere in its being.
— Spinoza, the *Ethics*

We belonged to two different castes of the
Nazi universe, and therefore when we spoke to each other
we were committing a crime, but we spoke anyway.
— Primo Levi, *Moments of Reprieve*

It was a bitterly cold day when Danielle and the children came
to live with us. The January frost was perceivable from their
crisp, ruddy complexions. The chill began to thaw almost immediately, however, and by the time coats, scarves, mittens,
and boots were cast off and put away in the closet, an almost
thermal sort of warmth seemed to be kindled among all of us.
The atmosphere was holiday-like. It was as though distant family members were reunited for a shared vacation, at maybe the

Ritz-Carlton or the Plaza, or maybe even a camping trip to the Rockies. There was an infectious sort of fervor and excitement germinating from the younger members of both families, but quickly spreading, like a wild fever, among all of us. It was as though this was a happening of some sort, a great unforgettable adventure that the two families were about to share, to embark upon together.

The first and foremost topic of conversation was the sleeping arrangements. Being a first-generation American, a child of immigrants, I had always been rather practical with my purchases. Each of the boys' beds had come equipped with a trundle bed, stashed neatly underneath. Our living room sofa opened up to a queen-sized bed, and we had a spare bedroom upstairs, which was frugally furnished with brick-and-board bookcases, a desk of two black metal filing cabinets with an oak butcher block slab on top (vintage of our medical/graduate school days), and our original wood frame bed (mattress on box variety), from the same common ancestry.

Joshua and Benyamen immediately began squabbling about whose room Leah would share. "She's really closer to my age," Joshua said, emphatically.

"No, she's closer to mine," Benyamen said, with equal emphasis.

"Actually, she's right in the middle between your two ages," I said, matter-of-factly, wondering to myself how this fact would add anything to help settle their dispute.

"But she'd be more comfortable in my room," said Benyamen, assuming a different angle. "It's bigger," he boasted, folding his arms in front of himself, somewhat conclusively, as if to say, "I rest my case," as though this argument held so much weight, all that the opposition could do was concede defeat.

"That's not fair," Joshua immediately rebutted, always one to defend his own rights. "You can't get the bigger room and Leah, too."

Leah seemed to enjoy being thought of as the prize, and grinned contentedly, an even bigger grin than usual.

"You know," I said thoughtfully, "maybe it would be best if Leah shared Joshua's room." You are growing up, Benyamen, and I don't know if an eight-year-old boy sharing a room with a six-and-a-half-year-old girl is entirely. . . ."

"Kosher," Danielle immediately interjected.

"That's right," I added, ". . . kosher."

So it was settled, then. Danielle would sleep in the living room, on the fold-out sofa, downstairs. Nicole, who was in that age of emerging womanhood, needed her privacy, and would have the spare bedroom upstairs. Leah would share Joshua's room, and Benyamen would share his room with Max.

"Ha ha," Benyamen suddenly lightened. "When you're deep asleep in your room, Max could teach me his magic tricks and I could do them all on you, Joshua."

In the midst of this fervor, people began settling in to their various rooms, unpacking, taking out old clothes from closets and drawers and stashing them in the cedar closet in the basement, making room by piling up thick bundles of old clothes inside chests, closets, and drawers, and finding hangers for the clothes of our guests.

Most of Danielle's and the kids' worldly possessions had been put in storage. They only took with them clothes and a few of their most cherished items. For Max, it meant his baseball card collection and sports memorabilia and a set of "Houdini's Best Magic Tricks." For Nicole, it was a set of *Vogue* and *Seventeen* magazines, along with a small corner drugstore's complete inventory of cosmetics. For Leah, it meant My Little Pony and Barbie dolls, and a musical jewelry box with a little ballerina that danced to the tune of "Edelweiss." For Danielle, it had been some important papers, which she carried with her in a small Gucci tote bag. In fact, all of their clothes were packed away in a matched set of Gucci luggage, a remnant of their former high-rolling life. I commented on how lovely the mauve and beige tweed baggage was, to which Danielle coquettishly remarked, "I know. I just don't have the right baggage for a homeless person! How does one dress to be a homeless person anyway?"

God Almighty, I thought to myself. *Would I have that presence of mind to crack jokes under those same conditions?* I was awestruck, once again, by her understated grace, her composure under such trying conditions, and felt that it was a shadow of her former life of ease, a sort of legacy of nobility that nothing, not even reality's hardships, could ever shake away.

When the bags were unpacked, we hauled them all off to the unfinished part of the basement for storage. All, that is, with the exception of the small Gucci tote bag, which Danielle asked if she might keep, out of view, but within easy access of her, between the sofa where she would be sleeping, and the wall that the sofa was up against. I saw no problem with that, as it was out of the way, and it seemed so important to her.

A few minutes later I was in the kitchen, cutting up vegetables for a chili, which was already on the fire. The scent of sautéed onions, garlic, and chili powder must have quickly drifted upstairs, because in a few minutes everyone had descended and congregated in the kitchen, like ants at a picnic.

"While you're in the kitchen," I said, turning to the little group, "I think I'd better lay out some ground rules. You know," I said, trying to assume a position of authority, which didn't come easily to me, "this is a kosher house." I opened up some of the white, oak trimmed cabinets. "The dairy side is here on the right. These red plastic dishes, these blue and yellow flowered Lenox ones, all these cups, mugs, silverware, Farberware aluminum pots, all these things on the right are dairy."

"And over here," I said, walking over to the left side of the kitchen, "all of these things are meat. The Dansk china, the blue every-day plastic, the good silver and the stainless in these drawers, these copper pots, here. . . ."

"Why do you bother with all this, anyway? Do you really think," Nicole interrupted, tossing with a flick of her head some of her thick mane of chestnut hair off her right shoulder, "do you really think it matters? Do you think this is going to get you into heaven any faster? Do you think God really cares if you keep your meat and your milk separately, like He's up there counting brownie points? What do you think this is, your ticket to salvation?" Her voice was somewhat sardonic, in the newly bitter way that only a 15 year old's can be.

"No, I don't," I answered her point-blank. "I'm not concerned at all about the world to come. I'm not even sure if there is one, to tell you the truth. I'm only concerned about this one."

"But you must believe God listens to your prayers before He does anyone else's, since they're said in Hebrew. You must feel you have a pretty cozy relationship with Him."

I looked at her honestly. "As a matter of fact, I have a very difficult time with that. I wish I didn't, but the truth is, I have a very hard time praying. It's hard for me to believe that He would listen to my prayers when He turned His back on so many others who prayed to Him in the same ancient Hebrew tongue."

"Then why do you do it? Why go through all this bother? It's all form and no content," she said, in a less scornful, but honestly inquisitive way.

"You're right, but . . . it's very complicated," I said, shrugging my shoulders, as if to say I wanted to dismiss it.

"Tell me," she said, "I'm really interested." She sounded concerned, this time, sincere.

"Well, basically I have two reasons," I began, candidly, unaffectedly, trying to avoid sounding like a college professor. "I don't know if there's a heaven, and frankly, well, I don't really care. Well, I do, in a different sense, but I don't observe the laws of Kashruth, or for that matter any laws, to get brownie points, to get my just postmortem dessert in the sky. Maybe children are motivated by rewards and punishment, but I can't honestly believe the idea of some big daddy in the sky handing out gold stars on foreheads, or smily faces, or inscribing one in the book of life, for that matter, is ever any motivation for any ethical conduct. I mean in any real sense."

"Well what do you think motivates ethical conduct, then, if it has nothing to do with God's will or an afterlife?" Nicole asked.

"Probably just basic empathy. The ability to put yourself in someone else's shoes. It's intuitive. We usually recognize the good or the right thing to do, immediately, and we just do it, kind of like a reflex act, kind of like breathing."

"Well, then, you still haven't answered my question. Why bother with these elaborate rituals of meat and dairy? What does this have to do with morality?"

"Probably nothing — or very little. But I do believe that, like Kohlberg, this psychologist at Harvard, whose done a lot of work on children and moral development, that for every act, there is a varying level of moral abstraction. Children at first are intellectually more concrete, and are motivated by immediate rewards or punishments. The *mitzvot* are like internalized rewards. But as they get more intellectually sophisticated, and are really able to abstract, reward and punishment — or *mitzvot* — mean progressively less and less to them, and its just the internalized, intrinsic act of helping. Just basic empathy, just being fully human, I guess."

"You still haven't answered my question," Nicole insisted. "What does this have to do with keeping two sets of dishes?"

"Well, not much, "I said matter-of-factly. "Except that like Kohlberg's belief in varying gradations of moral and intellectual abstraction, I also believe that there are varying levels of spiritual abstraction that depend on your ability for abstraction. The laws just sort of set the tone for higher levels of intellectual abstraction and, higher acts of ethical conduct and of empathy, or just basic acts of human kindness or of *Tikun Olam*, of healing of the world for no reason — just its own intrinsic sake."

"You mean," Nicole said, brushing off a wisp of gorgeous thick hair from her forehead, as she spoke, "you mean kosher people are so busy feeling guilty if they use a butter knife to cut their meat with, they can't move on from there, to worse sins, like murder?"

"Well kind of, but not exactly." We all laughed.

"But you didn't tell us your other reason," Max interjected, "You said you had two."

"Well, it's kinda complicated."

"Come on," Nicole and Max both chided in unison. "Spit it out."

"All right," I said, in a kind of conciliatory tone." It's just that" (I really felt pressed, at this point — I wasn't sure I really wanted to get into this, just now) "I don't want to . . . I don't want to," I stammered, "grant any posthumous victories to our enemies." I stared directly ahead of the little group, as I said this, at the oak and white kitchen clock with its large black roman numerals, trying, specifically, to avoid Danielle's azure blue gaze. I felt, somehow, cruel, insensitive, wrong, to bring this up just now. As though I was asking a handicapped child why he must always sit in that wheelchair.

Danielle excused herself, now, her face flushed. And a few minutes later, I could hear the sound of her throwing up, in the little pink powder room, off of the kitchen.

David had come home from work early that evening, and lit a fire in the fireplace, before we sat down to our chili dinner, which was served in a huge earthenware pot on our large country-style oak table. A general spirit of cooperation and cheer pervaded the house. The children all wanted to contribute something toward the smooth running of the house, just naturally falling into place, taking on various household tasks, like putting the dishes on the table, clearing them off, scraping leftovers into the trash, or into McDavid's bowl.

I had a difficult time falling asleep that night. The excitement of all the day's events wouldn't escape my brain. I just couldn't switch gears and relax. I slipped off of the bed gently, so as not to wake David, threw on a terry cloth robe, and went down to the kitchen. Danielle was there. She looked celestial in her soft, apricot brushed silk nightgown, her hair disheveled, her bare feet on the hardwood floor.

"Insomnia?" I asked.

"Yeah."

"Me too. Let's make some herbal tea. That might relax us a bit."

I took the kettle out. It was a white enamel one with delicately sketched lavender blue violets on it. The enamel was beginning to crack. It had the look of age.

"Nice kettle," Danielle commented. "Family heirloom?"

"No," I shrugged, with a wistful smile. "My family doesn't have any heirlooms."

"Oh . . . right," she said, with an embarrassed laugh.

The kettle whistled. I poured us both a cup of herbal tea, and watched as the tiny tea leaves slowly made their way to the top. We sat, down at the kitchen table, and quietly nursed our tea together.

"I have to say," Danielle said with an honest, fatigued expression on her face. "You've been fantastic. And I'm sure it's no coincidence that it has only been my Jewish friends who have really been there for me these last couple of months."

I just listened, as she went on, softly.

"It's been my friends from Washington Hebrew Congregation who have taken me shopping with them to MaGruder's

and just so happened to end up paying the bill, so they knew
my family would have food on the table, who have co-signed
the Hebrew Free Loan with you and David, who have invited
me and the kids over for Thanksgiving and Chanukah, who
have offered me housing in their attics or basements, who have
put me in touch with attorney-friends and advocates they knew,
socially, who would do just about anything for me.

"I don't think I could have survived without my Jewish
friends. I don't know," she continued, with a shrug. "I'm sure
there must be a message to all this, somewhere."

"I guess we're just experienced in the art of knowing how to
survive." We both laughed.

"But I don't know how anybody could go through a divorce, alone. People have been so wonderful. So many have
come through for me. It makes it hard for me to understand
why shelters for the homeless are filled with women and children who have been deserted by their husbands. Why are there
street people when people are so basically kind?"

"It's not so hard to understand, Danielle," I said, softly. "It's
not that people are so kind. It's that you awaken a certain kindness within people. You have a certain magnetism that draws
out the very best in a person, and then they feel good about
themselves, in turn."

"I don't understand. What separates me from the average
street person? We're both in the same straits. We're both destitute. Why don't they have that same 'magnetic' appeal?"

"It's not that difficult to understand, Danielle," I continued.
"There's no barrier between you and me. You're easy to relate to.
You're attractive, you're articulate, you're white, you're not scary
looking."

"Well plenty of the women that fill up the shelters for the
homeless fit that description."

"But it's more than that," I went on. "There's something
about you that kind of provokes an internal sense of justice. You

weren't made for this kind of suffering. I don't know. It's your upper class underpinnings showing through, I guess."

"Oh, I see what you mean . . . my upper class underpinnings," she repeated, still nursing her tea. Then, she put her cup down, raised her head heavenward, solemnly, as if in prayer, and whispered half-audibly, "Thank you, Vater . . . thank you."

Chapter 13

RADIANT ENERGY

Rejected by mankind, the condemned do not go so
far as to reject it, in turn. Their faith in history remains
unshaken, and one may well wonder why. They do not despair.
The proof: They persist in surviving, not only to survive,
but to testify. The victims elect to become witnesses.
— Elie Wiesel, *One Generation After*

The Holocaust was certainly a Jewish tragedy. But it was not
"only" a Jewish tragedy. It was also a Christian tragedy, a tragedy
for Western civilization, and a tragedy for all humankind. The
killing was done by people, to other people, while still other
people stood by. The perpetrators, where they were not actually
Christians, arose from a Christian culture. The bystanders most
capable of helping were Christians. The point should have been
obvious. Yet comparatively few American non-Jews recognized
that the plight of European Jews was their plight too.
— David Wyman, *The Abandonment of the Jews*

Things settled into a relaxing, comfortable rhythm at home.
I have to admit, I enjoyed the company of a woman friend in
the house. Someone with whom to linger an extra five minutes
over coffee, bagels, and conversation in the morning, before hit-
ting the glaring light of reality, and the rush-hour traffic on the
beltway. The rhythm of a woman's internal time clock is slower,
gentler, more reflective, like the ebbing tide of the sea. I couldn't
help but feel that all those years that I had tied myself down to
a nine-to-five schedule, that I had advanced up the administra-
tive ladder in my job, I was also denying a little part of myself,
trying to fashion myself into something I was not.

Oh, how nice it was to have another woman in the house,
someone with whom to snatch an extra five minutes with at
breakfast to leisurely browse through the Style section of the
Washington Post, and with whom to ogle at the back pages of
the *New York Times* magazine section on Sunday mornings,
where they listed the pricey estates from Sotheby's. Women
seem to innately know a lesson that men don't discover until
much later in life. It is a knowledge so intrinsic to women, it is
almost as though it emanates out of their creative womb. The
knowledge that every single moment needn't be productive or
goal-oriented. While men are hurrying off to erect steel and
concrete superstructures against huge urban landscapes, women
seem to be just as content to enjoy the quiet shared laughter
of a friend. They know that there should be time and space for
idle fantasy and for the gentle play of the imagination. They are
much more in touch with the child from within.

Yes, I was enjoying the company of Danielle, and I did
feel a potent sisterly bond toward her. I felt her vulnerability
against the male constructed labyrinth of the legal system. Yet
this bond did not prevent me from sneaking home from the
office a few minutes before her in order to check the black,
metal mailbox that stood between my yard and the driveway, to

see if a response had yet arrived to my inquiries to Los Angeles and Jerusalem. Hers was not the only bond to which I felt, and as potent as it was, it was not the most potent. The memory of what my father was and how he suffered, still, and would always, occupy the most regnant and essential part of my being. And so, the gnawing, throbbing thirst to find out the facts about Danielle's father's life did not dissipate. This sisterly bond I felt toward her only compounded the issue, intensifying my thirst, tugging away at my conflicting loyalties, and unleashing new tides of constant nagging headaches.

A few weeks after Danielle and her kids had settled into the house, I received a phone call from David at the office. "Rach," he asked, "is Danielle in the office, now?"

"No. She's out in the field, doing some testing. Why?"

"You'll never guess who came into the office today," he said, his voice impassioned with excitement.

David was a well-respected physician in the Washington area, a gastroenterologist. And in this stressful nation's capital, it isn't unusual for politicians and journalists and people of renown to cross his threshold. After all, life in the fast lane in this political mecca has its price, the first one being an irritating knot in the middle of one's stomach.

"I don't know . . . Ronald Reagan."

"No. It's someone you'd really admire."

"Daniel Patrick Moynihan . . . Jeane Kirkpatrick . . . Daniel Inouye?"

"No," David said, with a slight chuckle. "I'll relieve you of your suspense — Harry Weiss."

"Harry Weiss?" I said, returning his laugh. "Who's Harry Weiss? Is that a name I'm supposed to recognize?"

"Well, I suppose his name isn't exactly a household word, yet . . . not that it'll ever be — but his work is of vital interest to you."

"Who is he, already?" Now he had my curiosity piqued.

"He works for the United States Department of Justice. He is chief investigator for the Office of Special Investigations."

I couldn't believe what I was hearing. Would this connection somehow unlock the secrets that had been steadily eating away at me all these months? Does this mean I would finally get a reprieve from those constant, throbbing headaches?

"His office was responsible for the investigations that led to the extraditions of some of your favorite people," David continued.

"Like who?"

"Like Klaus Barbie . . . like Ivan Demjanjuk."

I already was in love with this man. I didn't care if he looked like a cross-eyed dwarf with a cleft palate.

"Why did he come to you? Is he seriously ill? Can I do something for him? He had already aroused my Jewish mother instincts, like a knee-jerk response, by the mere fact that he crossed the threshold into a doctor's office.

"It's nothing serious, just irritable bowel syndrome. I suppose if I had to deal with the level of humanity his office constantly deals with, on a daily basis, my bowels would start to react a little bit, too."

"You didn't ask him if he's ever heard of Danielle's father, did you? If he recognized the name?"

"Well, I didn't feel it was professional. I'm sure his work is strictly confidential. And I just didn't think it was appropriate for his doctor to go fishing for information."

"David! How could you? Why are you always so earnestly ethical?"

"Well, I just didn't feel right about it, Rach. But I do have his office number, if you want to call and introduce yourself, and explain the situation. See what he says."

"Thanks," I said, lukewarmly. I was sure his office was just going to give me the run-around.

"Hey, don't sound so indifferent. He told me some stuff which might be of some interest to you."

"Like what?"

"Like part of the reason he's under stress. He says he feels like he has just so much time before the Nazis living in the country just die of natural causes before the Department of Special Investigations has a chance to bring them to justice."

"So what else is new?" I said, my voice still somewhat dispassionate.

"Well, he said that the office has more work cut out for them than they have years left to do it, for the simple fact that there are so many Nazis who have been living peacefully in this country since the war."

"What are you telling me, David?"

"I'm only telling you what he told me. And that's just that there are literally hundreds of men who held high ranking offices within the National Socialist Party who have been safely granted asylum in this country."

"I don't understand what you're saying, David. They were our enemies. You're not trying to tell me that our government cooperated in letting these people in, are you?"

"Well, I'm only relaying what he told me, Rach. Apparently, many Nazis and their collaborators entered this country under assumed identities. The United States Department of State worked in cooperation with the Department of Immigration and Naturalization to issue them phony visas and to help settle them in this country."

The sound waves of his voice entered my auditory canal, but could not penetrate my brain. I felt like a child, standing by the road, watching her idol being slowly splashed with mud.

"What are you saying, David?" I asked, my voice, agitated.

"I'm just saying that he attributes a lot of his personal stress to the interagency roadblocks that have been put up against his department's work. Apparently, senior members of the State Department, the C.I.A., the Pentagon, and the Department of Immigration and Naturalization have had a lot invested in keeping this information hushed up. Apparently, everyone was willing to go along with it, at the time. He said the government is asking him to do his job with one hand, while tying the other behind his back."

"Why?" I asked, still incredulous. "What was in it for our government? They hated these people just a few short years ago, during the war!"

"Yes, but at that point the war was over, and we had a new enemy, some felt, a greater enemy, in the Soviet Union. You have to remember, Rach, that was the time of the Red Scare . . . McCarthyism. People in this country, not just the radical fringe on the far right, but the average American, hated Communists with a passion. There was almost a religious fervor about it. They were called Satan's army on earth."

"What does that have to do with letting Nazis in?"

"A great deal. At that time, America thought a war between the United States and the Soviet Union was imminent. Many of the officers of the Schutzstaffel, the SS, were in intelligence and knew a lot of information about the activities of the Soviets which was very valuable to our country, at the time. Plus, there was a nuclear weapons build up, there was a race to conquer space, we were still at war with Japan, there was the Cold War with Russia. America needed some of the scientists from Nazi Germany to address some of these new concerns."

"So the enemy of my enemy is my friend? Is that what you're saying, no matter who that enemy was or what he did?"

"Well, that seemed to be the feeling among some high ranking officials of our government, at the time."

"I still can't believe what you're telling me, David. You mean some of these people were actually involved in Nazi atrocities, in acts against humanity, and our government knew about it, and was willing to look the other way?"

"Exactly, according to Harry Weiss. He said that declassified U.S. Army records show that American intelligence officials, at the time, were clearly aware that they were recruiting many former Nazis, including officers from the Waffen SS, people who were known to have had participated in real atrocities, war crimes, enslavements, exterminations, deportations, murders, rapes, tortures — you name it."

"Oh, David. I'm really having a hard time with this information. Weren't they concerned that it might taint the moral character of our nation to have these sorts of monsters living among us?"

"Apparently that wasn't considered to be as great a threat as that of losing the Cold War."

"You mean they didn't care about justice?"

"Well, according to Harry Weiss, that just wasn't the prevailing concern of the time. He said a senior member of the Pentagon had advised the United States Army to change its files on some German scientists so we could bring them into this country with clean wartime records. He quoted a top Pentagon official, who said to stop "beating a dead Nazi horse.""

"David," I said after a painful pause, tears locked just behind my voice, waiting to burst out. "I can't believe this country which turned away Jews from its harbor in New York because they 'didn't have enough room' during the war, and sent them back to the concentration camps to die, suddenly had room for these Nazis."

"You mean the Spirit of St. Louis?"

"Yeah — and I mean the millions of Jews who could've escaped before the fall of 1941, when Hitler blocked the exits for them, had the United States lowered its immigration quotas against them. By the time the United States decided to make any effort, the doors on the European side were all tightly shut. And even then, the effort was minimal. It's all clearly documented in David Wyman's book, *The Abandonment of the Jews.*

"You're really hot about this issue, Rach."

"Damn it, David! Sure I'm hot about this issue. You would be too if your ancestors hadn't left Europe sooner. My parents might not have gone to Auschwitz if America had acted differently!" Now I was the one whose voice was laced with passion. I didn't care if they heard me all the way down the hall.

I continued, oblivious to the ascending volume of my voice. "Thousands of refugees would line up to the doors of the consulate, only to be turned away empty handed, and to eventually make what for many was their last journey to Auschwitz."

"Rach, I know. I'm on your side, remember? Hitler would have gassed me, too."

"I know David. It's just that these questions have always bothered me. And now, what you're telling me only increases my feelings of confusion about our country's less than pure motives during the war. Why didn't America carry out some sort of rescue mission? As soon as the operations against the Jews began, they received well-documented intelligence reports that the Nazis were systematically annihilating European Jews. These reports were made fully public by November of 1942. But President Roosevelt did nothing, and was just indifferent to these reports for about 14 months after that. Do you realize how many Jews were gassed in those 14 months? And why didn't Roosevelt bomb the gas chambers or the railroads leading to those gas chambers, when a large number of American bombing raids were taking place within a few miles of Auschwitz? I just can't believe it. And now you're telling me that they opened up those doors which had been so tightly locked against Jews . . . to Nazis?"

"Believe it, Rach. I guess Jewish blood was always cheap. Even in this country."

For the remainder of the day, I found myself plagued by the same questions that had constantly plagued me throughout my childhood, despite my continual, futile attempts to change my focus and move on. I found myself looking at all my fellow coworkers in the office, all "good" people in the conventional sense of the word, fellow psychologists, secretaries, administrators, mail carriers that came into my purview, and asking myself, *If the Holocaust were to happen today, where would you be? Would you be capable of escaping your ego-myopic universe enough to be able to feel the pain and suffering of another human being? Would this feeling be profound enough to shake off the protective womb of apathy that surrounds us all like a thick coating of amniotic fluid, swaddling us from self-sacrifice and personal risk?*

Sadly, sadly, my answer was always the same.

Chapter 14

FISSION

God may be sophisticated, but he's not malicious.
— Albert Einstein

How can anyone who recognizes the names Auschwitz
and My Lai, or has walked the corridors of hospitals
and nursing homes, dare to answer the question of
the world's suffering by quoting Isaiah: "Tell the righteous
it shall be well with them?" To believe that today,
a person would either have to deny the facts that
press upon him from every side, or else define what he
means by "righteous" in order to fit the inescapable facts.
— Harold Kushner,
When Bad Things Happen to Good People

I raced home from work that evening to check the mailbox,
which had become almost a ritual by now. My hands quickly
sorted through the junk mail, until they fell upon a slim blue

aerogram from Jerusalem. It was not, however, from the Yad Vashem Archives. It was from my sister Rivka.

I quickly tore open the aerogram, anxious to hear news of how my sweet sister and her little family were doing. She wrote:

Dear Rachel,

It is not easy for me to write this letter. Things were going very well for us, until a few weeks ago. The children are doing very well in school, Thank God. They're growing up to be so healthy and good looking, like two little Sabras. The problem is with me. I kept feeling tired, no — exhausted. So tired it was a major effort for me to lift Elona out of the bath, and to get down on the floor and play backgammon with Amir. I also had terrible headaches, so terrible all I wanted to do was go to bed, and put the pillow over my head, to block out all light, all sounds, all smells.

Rafi was sick of listening to me "kvetch" all day, and finally sent me off to Kupat Cholim for some tests. As soon as they had the test results they wanted to admit me, immediately, into Hadassah Hospital. I explained that I had two little kids, that they would be expecting me at home, when they came home from school. They told me to call some friends to arrange for coverage. That I might have to be in the hospital, overnight. I called my friend, Norit, the one I told you about whose husband is a physicist. She said not to worry, she would be there for Amir and Elona. She's such a doll.

Anyway, they wanted me to go into Hadassah immediately, for some blood transfusions. They still wouldn't let me know what the problem was. Rafi and I thought it might be my anemia. But then a resident on the floor told us. It's acute leukemia. I finally spoke to the doctor. He couldn't answer any of my questions. He refused to put a number on how many years I could live with this, saying so many of his patients have proven him wrong, it's not fair to put a number on it. Rafi kept pressing him, however. He finally said "the average" is maybe five years, but that I shouldn't look at myself as a statistic, but a human being, and to have "Bitachon," to have faith, there are always miracles.

I'm so scared. I keep looking at Amir and Elona. I know they're gonna need a mother there, to see them through life. My major goal right now is to fill them up with a core, a supply in the pit of their stomachs, of good mothering, of good memories of me. So that they will know that they're really special, and lovable. Anything else, if I can make it through the week, and put Shabbas on the table, is just an extra, a bonus.

I know HaShem has a reason for all this, but I can't understand what it is. I keep delving into my past, thinking that somewhere, somehow, I must have sinned. But I just can't think of what it is HaShem is punishing me for.

Please, Rach, I didn't tell you all this to worry you. It's just that you're my sister, and I love you so much, and I thought you had to know. My love to David and the boys.

Rivka

Oh Rivka, Rivka, Rivka — my sweet sister. How can this be? You're so good, so beautiful so pure. What is HaShem doing? Is this some sort of a sick, cruel joke He's playing on all of us, laughing up there in the heavens? If so, I didn't appreciate His sense of humor. For a moment, I felt like yelling, screaming at God. I would not allow myself. Like an instantaneous reflex, I remained mute, numb, muffling my anguish within my larynx, not allowing it to emanate into the cold January air. Instead, I felt my trembling hands still holding the thin blue paper of the aerogram, opening and reaching up toward the heavens, in that characteristic Jewish gesture of helplessness, of questioning, which, after so many centuries of wrestling with the role of Job, has been deeply inscribed within my genetic blueprint, and is now embedded within our collective physiology.

I crumpled up the letter, and stuck it in the bottom of my purse. I didn't know, quite yet, how to tell the kids. I decided not to discuss it around them, to put it on hold, until I could get my thoughts together about this, to be able to present it to the children in some sort of fashion which would not crumble this foundation of faith I was trying so hard to erect for them.

That evening went smoothly. David had to work late at the hospital, and Danielle and I and the kids had settled into a comfortable routine of preparing dinner together. I spent the evening repressing that malignant lump of anguish, still somewhere between my stomach and my larynx, waiting to erupt, and covering it up with a contrived smile and a false sense of bonhomie.

As the dinner preparations ensued, my mind raced quickly back to images of Rivka, my pure, golden sister, my childhood hero, with her halo only visible to me from my particular vantage point in my little universe. I remember how proud I was of her when I would wait by the flagpole after school, and she would pick me up, always surrounded by a coterie of friends, all older, smarter, attractive girls like herself. I remember all the little rituals she used to teach me, walking together to school, like not to step on the cracks of the sidewalk, and trying to master her well-developed skill of skipping and managing to avoid the cracks, at the same time. I remember how she was a wiz at the hoola-hoop and the Duncan yo-yo, the neighborhood champion at both, so perfect at everything she put her hand to. I remember how she once devised this game to manage to get me to eat (for I was the "skinny" one, the source of my mother's endless worry) by dressing up forks, as one would little paper dolls with hats fashioned out of food, and pretending the "fork-dolls" were going to the zoo, where the "big animals" would eat their "hats." The game stuck for quite some time. I remember the hilarious stories she used to create, much to my delight, of the "shtinky yiddishe madella," which would throw me into keels of laughter, long after the lights went out, and when we were supposed to be sound asleep in our shared bedroom. I remember how once, on a day that school was closed because of snow, I was not allowed out of the house because of a fever and she made me a miniature snowman that melted all over the olive green living room rug. And I remember how, on Shabbas morning, she would hurry to wake and dress early, to accompany my father on his walk to shul. And I remember how devout and earnest her prayers had been once she had arrived there. How could this be, the two purest souls of my childhood?

The dinner dishes cleared, the children safely tucked into their beds, I went down to the kitchen to share a cup of tea with Danielle, which had become a comfortable evening ritual. I watched the steam slowly emit from the white and lavender blue enamel kettle. It pressed against my face. I felt its hot wetness, mingling with my tears. Finally, I allowed the low, moaning sound which had been trapped within my larynx to escape upward into the vaporous atmosphere.

I felt Danielle's arm around me. "What's wrong, Rach?"

"Bad news from my sister, Rivka, in Israel. She has leukemia." I couldn't believe I was actually saying this, as though by allowing my lips to form those words, I was actually making this more of a reality.

"I'm sorry," she said gently. She could feel my anguish. I knew that.

"I just don't understand it. I just don't understand why God operates the way He does. Or why He allows things to happen the way they do."

"You have to have faith, Rach. There's always a reason. Even if its not immediately apparent to us."

"It's just so hard, Danielle. You never met Rivka. She was always so good, so gentle, so pure. Now she's punishing herself, delving into her past, trying to uncover what terrible sin it is that God is punishing her for. She never would hurt a fly! Her whole life was predicated by doing acts of goodness, of kindness and righteousness."

"God has His reasons. Maybe her illness is teaching someone about how to die peacefully."

"What are you saying, Danielle?" I wasn't quite sure I liked what I was hearing, and I certainly wasn't ready to hear about my sister's death, as though it was a foregone conclusion.

"I'm saying, maybe her illness has a reason. I don't know what it is. Maybe she will die a peaceful death, and by doing that, teach other patients with cancer how to go to their deaths in peace."

"Oh, God, Danielle. I don't want to hear this. I'm not ready to hear this. Why should her life be a pawn in some master chess game? What makes her life less valuable in this perverse, simplistic little Weltanschauung of yours than that of the next person who comes along?"

"I'm not saying that. I'm just saying that you have to have faith . . . Emunah. That's the word, isn't it?"

"You know, Danielle, things are not always so simple, so facile, as you'd prefer to see them. I'm really getting a little sick of your pat answers. What is your quick and easy little answer to the million and a half children who were murdered at Auschwitz, who were snuffed out like a candle, even before they had a chance to live?"

"There was an answer, and there is. I know there is. We just don't see it now. It's too close to us. Maybe in a few generations they will. Maybe on another planet."

"But why? Why did they have to march together to the gas chambers? So some future generation would profit from that piece of knowledge, that little homily at the end of that sad, sad chapter in history, like some little moral taped to the end of an Aesop's fable?

"You know, I am sick of hearing you talk about the Holocaust. You're obsessed with it. You have no right to talk about it. You weren't there."

"And were you? Where were you? I'm obsessed with the Holocaust? You know, hardly a conversation goes by when you don't make some reference or other to the Holocaust. Since when does this subject belong to you? Do you own it ?"

"Stop it, Rach! The Holocaust is my loss as well as yours! You have no idea what happens to me every time I hear the word "Holocaust." It's like having a deck of 52 cards spread out in front of my eyes, all with images of murders, rapes, gas chambers, skeletons piled up. I've lived with these horrible images my whole life! I'm sick of it! I'm sick of hearing about them!"

"Why, Danielle? Why have you lived with these images your whole life?" I felt a little cruel asking this question, but I wanted to hear what she had to say, once and for all. "And why are you sick of hearing about the Holocaust? *The Winds of War* is a best seller, now. *War and Remembrance* is due to be aired in the fall. Obviously, not everybody shares your feelings about the subject. Why do you feel this way?" I looked her squarely in the eye.

Her face reddened. "You have no right asking me this question! You have no idea how the German nation suffered because of the Holocaust."

"No I don't," I said quietly. "Tell me."

"Germany was always the seat of Western civilization — of philosophy, of literature, of music — Bach, Beethoven, Mozart, Wagner, Kant, Hegel, Humboldt, Mann, Hess, Goethe, Nietzsche, Schlegel, Schopenhauer. Then the Holocaust came. It was a tragedy, a tragedy for German civilization. I mourn for that nation, for the glory that was once Germany."

"Oh, really. It's funny. I have very little sympathy for the death of the German nation. I don't mourn for it at all. I mourn for the six million Jews that perished in the gas chambers. No one forced the German people to do that. And I mourn the pure part of humanity that died along with the six million Jews."

"Get real, Rachel! You have no understanding of what the German people were up against between the two world wars! They were impoverished, humiliated. And they looked and they saw all these wealthy Jews who owned banks and railroads living in their midst."

"I can't believe what you're saying, Danielle! Where did you get this from? This sounds like it comes straight out of the *Protocols of the Elders of Zion* or *Mein Kampf!* Do you really believe this stuff? Hitler didn't limit his creed of hatred to wealthy Jews. He hated all Jews, and the entire German nation was quick to pick up on that hatred and cooperate. There was even a board game named Judenrein that they used to give to children to play with. The first person to 'eliminate the Jewish vermin' from the 'pure Aryan board' was declared the winner."

"I'm just trying to explain why the Holocaust happened from a different perspective. The Germans had always been a proud people, and then they saw all these strangers living within them with so much. . . ."

"Are you trying to tell me that a Jew is less entitled to live comfortably than a Christian? And that that's a justifiable rationale for hatred — for genocide? Listen, I have news for you, Danielle. The wealthy Jews and the paupers and peasants all marched hand in hand together under the gates of Auschwitz!"

"That's not what I'm saying. I just don't think that you have any right to question God and His motives for things."

"Listen, Danielle. I'm just saying it's not so easy to have faith. You can't just swallow it down whole, like a pill."

"But you weren't there. You hide your cynicism behind this. Maybe you're just not capable of real faith."

"But my father was there — in Auschwitz. I once heard him talking to my mother. He said he had seen a Din Torah, a kind of legal, religious tribunal, that some rabbis had conducted. They were trying God. And at the end of a strong theological debate . . . God lost."

"They had no right to do that."

"What do you mean — they had no right to do that? They saw the world being turned upside-down and inside out, in front of their eyes. Innocent people, good people were dying, being tortured, mutilated, while evil people were prospering. That goes against everything they were taught. Everything they knew! How else were they to deal with it, to react?"

"You know, Rach. I'm the one that's getting sick now. You have no right to talk this way. You weren't there. And how do you know what your father did to survive under those conditions? How do you know he didn't sacrifice someone else's life for his? Some people say the best and the purest were the first to go to the gas chambers."

This was too much. Everything was so distorted and perverted. White was becoming black, in an instant, and black was becoming white. The whole world was being homogenized, distorted into her comfortable, delusional world view. I couldn't take it, and I couldn't take her. I got up and slapped her, one sharp, crisp slap against her cheek, which left a red imprint of my hand across her face.

"How dare you?" I asked. "I don't want you to ever say that again! You have no idea what it was like. You . . . you . . . Prussian Princess! It was like a roll of the dice! Like a crapshoot — who lived and who died. One survivor said she was almost gassed, but they didn't have enough room in the oven to close the door! How dare you? You . . . you ignorant little Wasp."

She looked at me, in shock, in stunned silence. "You just don't understand, Rachel. What I've had to live with my whole life. You wouldn't. You never could."

I really wanted to ask her what she knew about her father, what he did to survive during that insane time, how she knew he was so pure, so good, his hands so clean . . . or if what she's had to live with her whole life had to do with some deep dark, secret she was harboring. But I couldn't. I just couldn't. I wouldn't even try to penetrate through that tightly woven web of delusion. I don't know why exactly. Maybe I was afraid she would decompose in front of my eyes. Maybe I was afraid she would attack me. She had so much invested in her little myth — maybe her sanity.

"I guess," I said after a long pause, "we've found our mutual Achilles' heel," I said with a contrived little laugh.

"I guess. . . . I'll try never to talk about the Holocaust to you."

"Yeah. We've certainly found which subject to avoid."

We left for bed, quickly, with a contrived sense of being friends once again, of having closed the subject of our differences once and for all, and conclusively.

Secretly, we both knew that we hadn't.

That night I had another one of my nightmares. I dreamt I was running from the Gestapo. I was in a forest, with the Partisans. I had my children, Benyamen and Joshua, with me, and Rivka was one of my children. I was scavenging around the woods for food, wild berries, nuts, and sap from leaves to feed my children so that they could survive. The Gestapo found us. We were forced to come out of the woods with our hands up, reaching toward heaven in that characteristically Jewish stance.

David woke me. He said I was making strange sounds in my sleep, a low, deep moaning sound. I immediately recognized the description of the sound. It was the same sound that used to emit from my father's lips when he had his nightmares.

That night, in bed, I asked David to bring Harry Weiss's phone number home from the office for me.

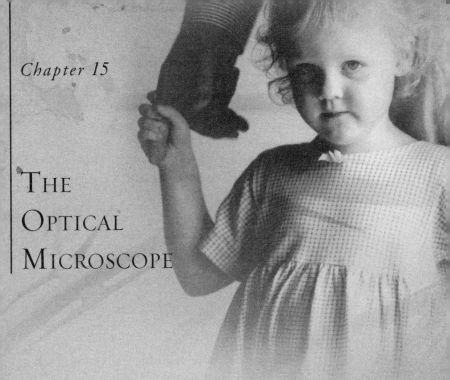

Chapter 15

THE
OPTICAL
MICROSCOPE

The SS guards took pleasure in telling us that we had no chance
of coming out alive, a point they emphasized with particular
relish by insisting that after the war the rest of the world would
not believe what happened, there would be rumors, specula-
tions, but no clear evidence, and people would conclude that
evil on such a scale was just not possible.
— A survivor of Dachau, as recorded in Terrence Des Pres'
The Survivor, An Anatomy of Life in the Death Camps

Human evidence must be preserved.
— Albert Camus

*T*he breakfast conversation was stilted. It was difficult for
me to interact normally, after last night. I looked at Danielle,
beautiful Danielle, still so thin, so delicate and vulnerable.
How I loved her. How I hated her. My best friend. My worst
enemy.

I could not wait until evening for David to come home with Harry Weiss's number. So that morning, as soon as we arrived at work, and Danielle was safely tucked away at work in another office, I dialed David at work, and quickly scribbled the number on a piece of yellow lined paper. Immediately, I dialed the seven digits, my heart pounding almost visibly through my white cotton blouse, as I listened to the ringing of the phone on the other end.

I was connected to his secretary. I explained that I was Dr. Stein's wife, and that this was a social call. She immediately put me through. The voice on the other end didn't exactly sound as though it belonged to Sir Galahad. It was thin, tinny, sounding like it hailed from some exotic planet, like Brooklyn. I introduced myself quickly as Dr. Stein's wife, and explained that I was interested in finding some information about an emigré from Germany, someone who had arrived here in 1945, who had been trained as a physicist and engineer in Berlin, and wanted to know if he just might happen to have a file on this man.

"Why do you want to know?"

"I'm curious. Just curious. I'm good friends with his daughter, and I just want to know."

"You know that our files are extremely confidential."

"I appreciate that. It's just that I have to know this. It's . . . it's very important to me."

"And what would you do with this information, once you got it?"

"I don't know. Probably nothing."

"Is this person alive?"

"Dead."

Long pause, then, "You know, whether or not the person is alive might or might not make it easier to release the information. Many of these cases are intermeshed with other cases. We have a whole team of attorneys working on these cases, and they do, too. If some of this information got leaked out to the general public, I'm sure it would work its way into their attorneys' offices, and a lot of cases would be thrown out on some sort of legal technicality."

"Who is the 'they' that you're referring to?"

"Some of Hitler's old buddies."

A sudden wave of terror overcame me at the sound of those words. Was I getting into something beyond my scope? In a flash, I pictured pounding, goose-stepping black leather boots coming after me, pounding at my door, and ordering me to pack my belongings into one suitcase, and be in the Stadtplatz in three minutes, to be ready for the next transport. I reoriented myself, quickly, taking a few deep breaths to regain my composure.

"Listen. I promise I will not reveal this to a soul. It's just that. . . . You can't understand how important this is to me. It's . . . it's. . . ." My voice had an imploring quality to it. I was afraid I sounded like a little girl. I hated my voice, just then.

"All right. Being that your husband is such a fine doctor and such a mensch. Meet me at the Justice Department, 14th Street entrance, tomorrow morning, 9:00 sharp."

The next morning I left the house early, explaining to Danielle that I had a gynecologist appointment in the District, and that I might take off the rest of the day, that I was desperately in need of a "mental health day" and would be using some of my untouched personal leave.

I must admit I felt sleuth-like, getting into my blue Volvo station wagon, and making the drive down 16th Street. These friends who knew me from my synagogue, my office, my neighborhood grocery store, would believe the nature of my covert mission? "Rachel Stein," I chuckled to myself, "Secret Nazi-hunter."

There is something galvanizing, almost electric, about this city, I thought to myself, as I was driving down there. The free capitol of the world. There is a certain high, a heady feeling, perhaps a hubris, that comes with living and working so close to so much power.

The White House came into full view in my windshield. A marvelous edifice, snow white, almost glowing, against the pale pinkish early morning winter's sky. And if there is any possibility of justice and compassion in any government, perhaps this is the place to find it.

I turned left down to 14th Street. Regal and dignified government buildings were interspersed with porn shops. Clean white and slate gray intermingled with neon lights and sleaze. Such a commentary on our humanity, on our potential for humanness. For every Raoul Wallenberg, an Adolph Eichmann. Living side by side in the same fragile little universe.

I found a meter on the street and fed it some quarters. Why were my hands sweaty and shaking, as I put the coins into the slots? Why was I trembling, as though I was coming close to an oracle? Wilhelm Von Hoffmann was dead. I wasn't going to exhume him from some cemetery in New Jersey, and bring him to justice. I just wanted to know the truth, and this was as close to the truth as I was likely to get.

It was exactly nine o'clock when I arrived on the steps of the Justice Department. It looked like an ordinary gray slate office building. Why was I expecting so many extraordinary things from it? I tried to wipe the sweat from my hands, inside the pockets of my winter coat.

A small, pot-bellied man with thining gray hair combed over to one side, as if to conceal the baldness, met me on the steps. Was this the great conveyor of Truth and Justice? My oracle, my King Arthur? The person responsible for extraditing Klaus Barbie and Ivan the Terrible? I could look directly into his eyes. He was nearly as short as I was.

He came over to me and introduced himself. He definitely seemed much less foreboding in person than he did over the phone. We walked together down the long marble corridor to his office.

We entered his office. It looked as though it had been tastefully furnished once by a decorator, but had since then been lived in many years, used and abused, by someone whose life was too cluttered to pay any attention to the details of tidiness or aesthetics. Piles of folders lay on his desk, gathering dust. He had two black metal baskets, one marked "in," the other marked "out," each with over a foot of unopened mail.

He sat back on his reclining chair and put his feet up on his Chippendale desk. My eyes quickly surveyed the room for the names on stray manila files. No such luck. Nothing was visible from my vantage point.

"So?" He finally said, after a long pause. "What brings you here?"

"I thought I explained it to you, yesterday, over the phone. This German physicist and engineer?"

"Yes, yes. I know all that, but why? What does it matter to you — you said he's dead."

"What do you mean, 'what does it matter?' I'm not sure I understand."

"Well the war was over 40 years ago. Most of the Nazis are either dead or peacefully dying of old age."

"I know that, but it's very important to me to find out about this person. I need to know."

"Why? Why is it so important to you? Why don't you just let the old Kraut rest in peace? What difference does it make?"

"It's important to me because of who I am."

"And who are you?"

"Rachel Stein. Daughter of Benyamen and Miriam Feld, both survivors, from Birkenau and Auschwitz."

"Hmmm. I see. And who is this woman, to you . . . this friend of yours?"

"She's my intern. I'm a psychologist. She's told me a great deal about her father. That he came from a high military family in Germany. That he was a member of Hitler Youth. That he was trained as a physicist and engineer. That he came over in 1945, but she believes that his hands were pure," I recounted.

He laughed, the laugh of an astute old age, who has heard one story too many. "They all say that," he said. "Nobody in Germany was responsible for the Holocaust. It just happened. Divine intervention."

"So . . . you want to know about a certain individual. Who did you say it was?" He was so calm, so aloof. Was he toying with me?

"I didn't yet. Hoffmann, Wilhelm Von Hoffmann. In America, he called himself William Hoffman, and dropped the extra 'n.'"

"What do you expect to do with the information? This is the Department of Justice. He's dead and buried."

My face was getting flushed. He was teasing me, I knew that. He might not even give me a bone to chew on. "I know. I know. It's too late for that."

"Then, what does it matter?"

Now I was getting angry. I had nothing to lose. He was just going to play with me. I might as well reveal my baser, less demure side, and unleash some of this tension. "What do you mean? What does it matter? Does anything matter? Does the truth matter?"

"Does it?" He smiled. He was enjoying this little cat-and-mouse game. And I, obviously, was not the feline.

"Does the truth matter?" I repeated. "Why are history books written? To record lies and illusions? Why do archaeologists and anthropologists dig up relics of the Incas, the Mayan the Byzantine and the Holy Roman Empires? What happened in the past does matter, otherwise there wouldn't be so many people devoting their lives to scholarly pursuits to uncover it. I didn't invent these disciplines, you know."

"You know, you're cute when you get angry."

How I was beginning to despise this sexist old creep, who, at this point in my mind, seemed to assume all the finer characteristics, both physical and moral, of the Vita Herring Maven. What was I wasting my time here for, anyway? I felt as though I had just lost my chance of winning a million dollar lottery by one single digit. I wanted to get out of there, fast. He's just going to tease me. I looked around at the putty gray metal file cabinets covering the space of one entire wall, filled to the brim with files of ex-Nazis, probably, mostly, at large. Some of them living out their golden years in nice Jewish neighborhoods like Miami and Scottsdale.

I thought I might give it one last shot. "Please. Don't give me that nonsense about it being 40 years, that the past is dead and buried. Forty years is just a blink of the eye when it comes to the life-span of civilization on our planet. As a psychologist, I predicate my whole life on the fact that we've got to come to terms with our pasts. And the first step to that is knowledge."

"Please, please. Next you'll go quoting Santayana to me. Spare me the lecture. I know, I know. You know you're preaching to the choir, don't you? I'm one of those that's working to get these monsters out of this country."

He interrupted himself for a moment and began to examine my face, intently, as though he was beginning to discover something in it he had, up until now, overlooked, maybe a lost part of himself. I noticed that his eyes were quite large, they had an honest glimmer in them, but that they had been buried under years of creases. For the moment, while he was examining me, they took on a different quality, seeming to widen with interest. "I'm sorry," he continued, "I hope I haven't come across as too cynical. Sometimes I think I've been working in this place too long. It's just that I know too much."

"Tell me about it," I said, trying not to sound too much like a psychologist.

"I know too much. Far too much for a nice Jewish boy, coming from the little 'shtetl' of Brooklyn. Too much for any one person to handle. Volumes could be written about what I have sitting here in my file cabinets — tomes."

"What can I say, Rachel? Rachela. May I call you that?" He continued, oblivious to my somewhat guarded response. "History books should be written about what I have here. I have classified information about murderers and atrocities. You wouldn't believe. No one would believe. Such a level of 'ben adon.' " He clasped his hand over one side of his balding forehead, and nodded his head back and forth, in a distinctly Jewish fashion, like someone praying over a gravestone of a lost loved one.

"But," he continued, "I wanted this job. I was once like you. I was young once, too. I asked for this position. I wanted truth. I wanted justice. Justice?" He laughed a weary little laugh to himself. "That's what my whole life was predicated upon . . . once."

He continued to study my face, intently. "But the truth?" he continued. "The truth is that the wheels of justice turn too damned slowly. Slower than the biological life span of the human animal." He paused, picking up a gold Parker pen and studying it, in his hand. "We have scores of Nazis living right here in this country, who are dying out natural deaths, who are being treated in hospitals and nursing homes by nice young Jewish doctors, like your husband, who are oblivious to their pasts." He jerked the pen down on his desk. It ricocheted off the desk and fell to the floor. "Frustration is too neat and simple a term for what I feel on this job . . . daily."

He leaned forward and continued to examine me with those tired, old eyes. "You want truth?" he asked.

I nodded.

"You promise you will never divulge any information that you get from this office?"

I promised.

"You are aware that if any of this ever gets out, not only may I lose my job, but some of them will never go to trial?"

I told him I was.

"You never met a Harry Weiss. Do you understand?"

I told him I had never seen him before in my life.

"Go." He gestured with his left hand toward the wall with the files. "Be my guest. I'll tell the secretary you have complete security clearances." He looked at his watch, quickly, and said, "I have a conference, down the hall." Then, he looked at me as though he was abandoning his belief in the Hellenic myth of Zeus, ruler over the high Titanic court of justice, in exchange for that of Aristotle, seeker of truth. "Go," he said in half disgust, "go have yourself a picnic."

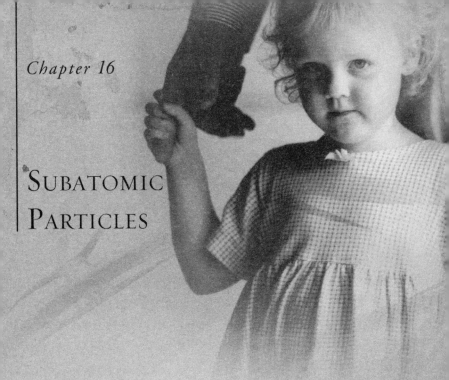

Chapter 16

SUBATOMIC
PARTICLES

It is true that totalitarian domination tried to establish
these holes of oblivion into which all deeds, good and
evil, would disappear, but just as the Nazis' feverish
attempts, from June 1942 on, to erase all traces of the
massacres, through cremation, through burning in open
pits, through the use of explosives and flame throwers and
bone crushing machinery — were doomed to failure, so
all efforts to let their opponents "disappear in silent
anonymity" were in vain. The holes of oblivion do not
exist. Nothing human is that perfect, and there are simply
too many people in the world to make oblivion possible.
One man will always be left to tell the story.
— Hannah Arendt, *Eichmann in Jerusalem*

The crime of the Germans is truly the most abominable
ever to be recorded in the history of so-called civilized nations. The conduct of the German intellectuals — seen as
a group — was no better than that of the mob. And even

now there is no indication of any regret or any real desire
to repair whatever little may be left to restore after these
gigantic murders. In view of these circumstances I feel
an irrepressible aversion to participating in anything that
represents any aspect of public life in Germany.
— Albert Einstein (when asked to renew official ties with
the Kaiser Wilhelm Institute, renamed the Planck Institute)

I stood in awe before the row upon row of metal filing cabinets,
a virtual wasteland, as if I were within grasp of seizing upon the
Holy Grail. Where to begin?

My hands shaking, I slowly opened one metal door, taking
out one file at a time, at random, and reading, very slowly.

Bruno Djantukovi, 88. Entered the United States in 1948,
a naturalized citizen of Chicago, had been the former Interior
Minister of the Nazi puppet state of Croatia, during World War
II. Known as the "Butcher of the Balkans," was extradited from
the United States in February of 1986, after losing a long legal
battle spanning four decades. Was awaiting trial in Yugoslavia.
Was recently cited as living in Paraguay by the Israeli Mossad.

Hans Schroeder, 79. Entered the United States in 1945
under the alias Saul Friedman. A naturalized citizen from Min-
neapolis, later moved to the retirement village of Sun Valley,
Arizona. Accused of serving in several Death's Head Battalions
of the Nazi SS at Majdanek and Auschwitz in Poland, and later
at the Flossenbuerg camp in Germany. Deportation proceedings
are beginning.

Bruno Werner, 82. Entered the United States in 1945. A
resident of Arlington, Virginia, was granted immediate citizen-
ship upon entering the country. Has been employed by the CIA
ever since. A high ranking member of the Gestapo. Responsible
for the deportations and mass murders of hundreds of thousands of Jews and other "undesirables." A note was inserted into

the file, asking that extradition proceedings be dropped, signed by the office of the director of the CIA.

Pieter Schimmer, 75. Joined the Einsatzkommandos in 1942. Later became SS commandant of the Przemysl forced labor camp in Poland and of the Rozwadeva ghetto. Employed by the CIA, is a long-time resident of Bethesda, Maryland. Extradition proceedings are beginning.

Reinhardt von Stauffenberg, 87. A member of the Sonderkommandos and the Waffen SS, joining in 1938. Personally developed and administered the notorious gas truck execution program which took the lives of approximately 250,000 people, most of them Jewish women and children. Was employed by NASA, in the rocket designing division. Retired to Pacific Palisades, California. Extradition proceedings have been in process for two years, and a longer legal entanglement is expected.

The pounding of one of my migraine headaches was beginning, as was this not so very faint wave of nausea. I didn't know how much more of this I could take. Knowing I could not walk away until the real objective of my mission was completed, I opened the drawer marked "V," and found a thick file toward the end of it marked "Wilhelm Von Hoffmann." I noticed a pad of yellow lined paper on Mr. Weiss's desk, and began taking notes.

On the front page of the file was a big red stamp, with the words INACTIVE. Brought into this country in 1945, Von Hoffmann was put to work in a highly secretive rocketry program at Wright Field, near Dayton, Ohio. By 1950, he was working for Bell Laboratories, in the aerosystems division, in New Jersey. He was a corporate expert in liaisons with U.S. military agencies. He had received high U.S. security clearances, and many public honors including the American Rocket Society's Astronautics Award.

Von Hoffmann had been one of the first to realize the potential of missiles for the work of the Third Reich, and began his work for the National Socialist Party in 1932. Apparently, there had been a bureaucratic battle with the SS over funding, engineers, and slave labor, for this project. Later in the war, in 1942, he had received a private audience with the Führer, showing him films, little wooden rockets, and other audio-visual aids, to convince Hitler to make Von Hoffmann's secret weapons a priority.

Von Hoffmann convinced Hitler to authorize the creation of a gigantic underground factory near Nordhausen for the mass production of his missiles.

I heaved a slight sigh of relief. It was not as bad as I had imagined. He was a scientist, working for the Third Reich, but after all, what choices had he in those bizarre and twisted times? I turned a page, and read on.

A document, written in German, and marked with the stamp of the Third Reich, was inserted into the file. It said that the Nazis were to use slave labor from the adjacent Dora concentration camps. Over 20,000 of them, many of them talented engineers, were to be selected.

Another document was inserted indicating that Von Hoffmann himself had overall jurisdiction over production schedules, including the amount of missiles to be built and the mix of the various models, signed by Heinrich Himmler, head of the SS.

The SS documented in the next page that in fewer than 15 months, it was able to get Dora's inmates to hack a huge underground production facility out of an abandoned salt mine near Nordhausen. The starvation diet and heavy labor generally killed the workers after a few months.

I turned another page and read how the laborers who actually made it into the facility fared. I saw after a minute that they were no better off than the others.

The Nazis were nothing if not meticulous in their record keeping. Another document, in fastidious, exacting micrography, recorded the names, prison numbers, and causes of death of the prisoners who died or were killed in the course of the project. For at least 20,000 of them, "cause of death" was listed as execution, starvation, or disease.

Oh, God, the pounding, the pressure in my mind gripped me . . . the nausea! How much of this was the result of the influence of the SS, and how much of this was because of the direct influence of Danielle's father? I knew that he was responsible for setting the work schedule, the production orders, and, apparently, he was an enthusiastic overseer, an eager taskmaster.

A letter to the SS with Van Hoffman's signature on it was for the demand of more and more slave laborers, that he was increasing production. Apparently, he had an increasing demand for more and more rockets, probably even more than there was fuel to launch — until the end of the war.

A letter from the SS indicated that the supply of food for the prisoners at Nordhausen had run out in February of 1945, but production orders were increasing, despite that lack of nourishment for the slave laborers. The letter went on to document how thousands of the laborers starved to death, how rampantly cholera ravaged the camp, how the SS had initially tried to cremate the bodies, but how the ovens could not keep up with the demand, so the corpses of the bodies were simply piled up to rot.

The pounding, pounding on my brain was getting to be too much. Everything became blurry for a moment. The nausea was traveling upward. I thought I was going to pass out or throw up, or both. I struggled to contain myself enough to read on.

There were slides from a documentary inserted into the file. I immediately recognized those pictures. They were images indelibly engraved on my brain. It showed living cadavers, virtual skeletons, leaning out of filthy bunkers to meet the American liberating army. It showed piles of corpses with no flesh, their flesh being eaten away through starvation. Then, there was a picture of an American soldier walking away in disgust. These shots were taken at the missile production factory at Nord-hausen in April of 1945. The Nordhausen plant and the Dora concentration camps were the first to be liberated by the U.S. army, and the first visual glimpses the American public saw of the concentration camps. I had seen them, known them, from a yearly screened Holocaust documentary. They were the stuff of my childhood nightmares.

There was almost an audible banging on my brain, now. Could Von Hoffmann have requested adequate rations for the prisoners? Could he have shut down the factory at Nordhausen on some technicality? Could he have cut down on production orders, rather than constantly speed up on them, at least to a level that the Third Reich was actually capable of launching?

At the bottom of the file was a letter signed by the office of the director of the Central Intelligence Agency, saying Von Hoffmann was the sort of Nazi who was "totally innocent" of any Nazi war crimes, he was simply a scientist doing his job, and how he was the ideal sort of German to recruit into this country, because of his scientific and technical expertise, since the war was over. The date on this letter was April 18, 1945.

I crumpled up the yellow lined paper, stuck it in the bottom of my purse, and tried to repress the dizziness, the banging on the brain, at least I could make the trip back up 16th Street to my home.

Chapter 17

INERTIA

Did anyone tell you, you're my hero? You're everything I ever dreamed that I could be. Did anyone tell you you're my hero? You are the wind beneath my wings.
— Henly and Siblar,
"The Wind Beneath My Wings"

Man tries to make for himself in the fashion that suits him best a simplified and intelligible picture of the world: he then tries to some extent to substitute this cosmos of his for the world of experience, and thus to overcome it. That is what the painter, the poet, the speculative philosopher, and the natural scientist do, each in his own fashion. Each makes this cosmos and its construction the pivot of his emotional life, in order to find in this way the peace and security that he cannot find within the all-too-narrow realm of swirling personal experience. The supreme task of the physicist is to arrive at those universal elementary laws from which the cosmos can be built upon from pure deduction.

There is no logical path to these laws; only intuition, resting
on sympathetic understanding, can lead to them.
— Albert Einstein

The imagination may be compared to Adam's dream —
he awoke and found it truth.
— Keats

I managed to repress the constant bang banging against the right
side of my brain, like the pulsating marching of goose-stepping
black leather boots, and maneuvered my Volvo down through
the establishments of sleaze interspersed with those of respect-
ability, like a checkerboard of filth and federal chic, which make
up our nation's capital. I felt, for a moment, like saying *Yizkor*,
the prayer for the dead, over the democratic ideal, and for its
vulnerability to human weakness.

Homeward bound. Home. Home. Home. Into the fresh,
clean, whitewashed air of the suburbs. But home was not where
I could find any peace, any reprieve from my constant, throbbing headache. There was nowhere to escape. Danielle was now
a constant part of my life. And I had let her into my life, in a
stronger sense than I cared to acknowledge. She was part and
parcel of every aspect of my life now, at home, at the office. I
shared meals with her. I shared my roof with her. I shared my
professional and personal secrets with her. I had given more than
just a little piece of myself to this . . . this daughter of a monster.

What to do? Where to run from her haunting, beautiful vis-
age? Oh, Daddy, Daddy, I prayed silently, how I need you, now.
How I wish you were here to guide me, with your silent, gentle,
Talmudic wisdom. Oh, how I wish you were here to guide me
through this conflicting enigma of twisted devotions that span
across continents and decades . . . and is shredding the fibers of
my heart into tiny bits.

My heart raced back to snatches of memories of my father, like faded snapshots in a worn family album. One of my most cherished of all of them, worthy of a solid gold frame, was the walk we had once shared together in a remote little park in Beit Hakerem, a gentle, quiet neighborhood in Jerusalem. The air was damp with spring. Children were playing hopscotch and singing *"Ani Rakevet"* (I am a choo-choo train) in the foliage in the background. I was confused. I knew I loved David, with all of the intensity of my being. I had felt his love for me. But we were young. Our brains and our plans for the future had not yet adjusted to these new tugs from our hearts. He never mentioned a future. And I was scared to utter any words that he was not yet ready to hear. I let loose all of my cares to you, Daddy. And you put your strong, gentle arms around my back, and comforted me with your tender voice of wisdom, with your few but well-chosen words. Straight from *Pirkei Avot*, the Teachings of the Fathers: "That which is not solved with words, is solved with time." This memory almost calmed the throbbing in my brain. Almost eased away the nausea, for a moment. Oh, Daddy, oh *Tataleh*. How I wish you were here, now, to walk me through this muddle. What would you do if you were in my shoes, now?

How I recognized the rhythm of those words. This constant refrain to the wisdom of a dead father, to guide us through our conflicts, like the comforting chant in a synagogue of the Rohanem, the high priests giving their priestly blessings, or a somniferous lullaby soothing away our nightmares. Hadn't I heard them before, someplace else?

Yes, the familiarity of the refrain to a dead father. It was Danielle's voice that I had recognized. Oh, poor Danielle. Suddenly a total sense of compassion overtook me. What does she have? Does she have any of these same comforting memories of her father? Can she place her memories in a solid gold frame, or has the frame been tarnished, blackened by other images, images she would like to blot out of her memory — out of all of our collective memories? Oh, poor, poor Danielle. You are truly an orphan, a sad, tragic orphan with a questionable legacy.

And what, what if she knew, all along, the truth about her father? What if this stuff she constantly preached about the "purity of his hands" was all an illusion? What did it matter? Maybe she knew it was a myth, on some level, but she needed it, the way we need our stories of the serpent talking to Eve in the Garden of Eden, or of God splitting the Red Sea in half for the children of Israel to cross it, kind of wanting so much to believe that this was the way it really was on some level, and kind of feeling somewhere, on another level that maybe, possibly, it just wasn't.

As we ease our children into slumber with these sweet, somniferous myths, we envy them a bit over their wide-eyed acceptance of these stories. We yearn to return to that earlier phase of innocence. And gradually, in a forced effort to preserve this innocence, these myths become ossified, solemnified, beneath centuries of rituals, like a precious newborn infant wrapped tightly in a swaddling cloth. They become the collective fairy tales of a social group, a sort of cultural chromosome, defining our version of "reality," and membership into our social groups, often through symbols of the myths worn around the neck with gold or silver chains — crosses, Stars of David, crescents. For some of us, our whole lives become predicated upon this premise of faith. The different symbols that we choose to wear around our necks do not really represent so vast a difference between us. They are simply different myths, different expressions of a similar premise, representing our fragile, finite attempts to understand our origins, and to display our devotion to that origin. And those who admit to not accepting these myths whole on some basic level, and who might even merely admit to the fact that they are built upon premises, and nothing more than premises, are deemed apostates, iconoclasts *"apikorsim,"* and often face excommunication from their social group.

In the end, our myths might be all that we have to pass down to our children. They're metaphors, illusions about that which we don't know, about that which is behind the visual world, probably containing glimpses of truths and untruths, fastened together with the fragile scotch tape of desire, of the will to believe, to create a sort of collage of a reality we would like to hope is really out there, so that we can all be eased, gently, gently, to sleep, and chase away all our nocturnal horrors.

And what if her reality, the legacy she had been handed down by her father, had been so terrifying, so horrible, so revolting and intolerable to her, that she had to depart from this reality a bit to refashion her story, to edit her mythology, to remake her hero? The heroes we choose probably reflect more about ourselves than about themselves, or about whom we would like to become. Their stories are often the scenarios we play out with our lives. Would I do any different, if I had to walk in her shoes? If I had inherited this kind of a sordid legacy?

Did it matter? What did it really matter? Danielle had taken on the vows and responsibilities of being a member of the Tribe of the Israelites, now. She had converted. She was now one of us. Her symbol was now the Star of David, worn always, around her neck. And her children were now just as much at the mercy of some raving anti-Semite, of some ranting, racist lunatic, as were my very own.

I only pitied her. She lacked, and so desperately sought after, the one thing which I had always had, and had always taken for granted — the legacy of purity of hands. *Pirkei Avot.* The Ethics of the Fathers.

I reached the house, and pulled my Volvo into the garage, knowing immediately what I had to do. I pulled the key out of the ignition and ran into the house, upstairs to my bathroom, finally ready to release my bile, retching and heaving all the way. Once in the bathroom, I reached for the yellow sheets of paper in the bottom of my purse, and tore them into tiny shreds. I leaned over the toilet and threw them in, throwing up all over them. They swirled down the white enamel drain of the toilet, painting a bright yellow whirl as they mixed with the greenish bile of my vomit.

Chapter 18

STATIC CONSTANTS

Today I am as old as the Jewish race. I seem to myself a Jew
at this moment. I, wandering in Egypt. I, crucified. I, perish-
ing. Even today the mark of the nails. . . . I am also a boy in
Belostok, the dropping blood spreads across the floor, the
public-bar heroes are rioting in an equal strength of garlic
and drink. I have no strength, go spinning from a boot,
shriek useless prayers that they don't listen to; with a cackle
of "Thrash the kikes and save Russia!" the corn chandler is
beating up my mother. . . .
I seem to myself like Anna Frank to be transparent as an
April twig and am in love. I have no need for words, I need
for us to look at one another.
— Yevgeny Alexandrovich Yevtushenko, *Babi Yar*

All we are given is possibilities —
to make ourselves one thing or another.
— Jose Ortega Y Gasset

There was a steady trickle of water dropping against the drain pipes in the yard from the icicles thawing in the early spring sun. Tiny green buds began to form on the brown, bony branches of the trees. There was a sweet sonorous song of sparrows in the early morning air. The migraine headaches began to gradually dissipate, as I felt the mystery of Danielle's legacy had been resolved. David alone, trustee of all my private confidences, shared my secret, as he had shared them all since we had met so long ago, a proven, steadfast rock of trust, his steady shoulders never wavering beneath the burden of my private thoughts. My intuitions on that April day in Jerusalem had been so right, so many years ago.

Meanwhile, a strong, more than sisterly bond began to form between Danielle and myself. Our distinct dialects melted into a lively sort of patois. There was an almost staccato-like, upbeat rhythm in the house. Rituals and responsibilities were shared. Dinner preparations became a lively, animated time. One layering the lasagna, one cutting up the tomatoes for the salad, as the children bustled in and out of the kitchen, stealing snatches of snacks from the fridge and snatches of our attention with little anecdotes of their day in school. I really enjoyed the company of Danielle and her children, in an almost ineffable way. The autonomy, so typical to middle-class, middle-age American suburban living, now, had melted away. I was almost beginning to dread the time that she would pack up her mauve and beige tweed Gucci baggage and leave. It was a harmonic time for us all.

There seemed to be a gradual transformation in the children during this time, particularly visible in Max's appearance. Friday evening was always special, the one time that David was certain to be home for dinner. I watched as Max's Friday evening costume changed from his Banana Republic shirt and well-worn jeans, to a white Polo shirt and olive khaki paints, to a white starched cotton oxford, and black tailored trousers. David had begun taking a special interest in Max, teaching him the HafTorah, the portion of the Torah for his Bar Mitzvah. And I noticed how Max would often say things, looking shyly out of the corner of his eye, for David's glimmer of approval.

Saturday mornings, David, the kids, and I would walk to our modern Orthodox service, while Danielle and her kids would take the car over to Washington Reform Congregation. This had all become part of the steady rhythm of the house.

One Saturday morning, David and I awakened early to the typical strains of a mother-adolescent daughter tug of war.

"I am not going! I am sick of Washington Reform. I am sick of those JAPpy girls with their perfect perms and their perfect manicures!"

"You are going. You have to, Nicole," Danielle answered with maternal resolve.

"Why? Why do I have to?"

"Because I'm your mother, and I say so."

"But Mom, that doesn't answer my question. Why do I have to go to synagogue every Saturday. It's so boring!"

"Because you're Jewish, and it's part of being a Jew. Nobody ever promised you that being a Jew would be easy."

"Oh, Mom. Will you stop with this act, already?"

"What act, Nicole?" Her voice was subdued.

"Will you stop making me into something that I'm not! I'm no more Jewish than Mother Teresa!"

"What are you trying to say, Nicole?" I heard Danielle's sober tone through the crack in my bedroom door. The shock waves in her voice penetrated upstairs, and invaded our bedroom, up through the wooden planks in the floor.

"I'm trying to say that I'm no Jew — and neither are you, Mom. Cut the act. I know the truth about you and about our lovely little family in Berlin!"

This was followed by the sound of the slapping of flesh, the slamming of doors, and the pounding of feet. A sound not altogether unfamiliar to the history of our people.

Some cacophony had invaded our harmonic little scene of family bliss.

Saturday afternoons, we would all have lunch together. Afterwards, David and Max would go into the living room together, and go over Max's HafTorah. Benyamen, Joshua, and Leah would retreat into their fantasy play world, together. Sometimes taking all the pillows and blankets from the bedrooms, and making the stairs into a pirate ship. (Benyamen was always the captain; Leah, the first mate; and Joshua, the skipper.) Or they would play outside, on the brown, wooden swing set in the backyard, sometimes pretending the club house that was connected to the swing set was a haunted house, sometimes, a rocket ship. McDavid assuming the roles of sea urchin, space alien, or ghost, respectively.

I had noticed how pretty Leah was becoming. She was beginning to take on some of the grace and charm of her mother, sometimes raising her eyebrows in that sagacious manner of hers, so appealing on such a young, pure face, in an almost comical way. She was at that stage, where she liked to try on her mother's make-up and jewelry. I noticed that her favorite one of all, the one she begged most often to wear, and which her mother would finally, after a wearying battle, often give in to, was Danielle's 24-karat gold Star of David.

Danielle and I would retire to the family room, the room with the southern exposure, and therefore the sunniest in the house. Little particles of dust would glimmer through waves of light streaming in through the glass panels of our French doors, in well-defined patterns. Tucked under our arms would be a well-worn book by some fine contemporary female novelist, Joyce Carol Oates or Ann Tyler, perhaps. We would snuggle up to our novels, sometimes wrapping ourselves in a cozy old afghan with frayed ends, retreating into the kitchen every now and then to pour ourselves cups of Earl Gray or Constant Comment tea out of the white enamel kettle with the blue-violet flowers.

And off alone, in a remote corner of the house, was Nicole, her radio blasting to the strains of Whitney Houston, as she carefully studied the glossy, white pages of a *Seventeen* or a *Glamour* magazine, as though it had been a cherished, old Gemarrah.

Thus we passed our Sabbath afternoons.

Chapter 19

Erosive Forces

This is the undramatic, unglorified sorrow of the body, a permanent part of the human condition which most of us prefer to ignore in favor of "inner" suffering — as if mind and body were separate worlds. But pain which goes on and on seeps through body and mind, and in this as in other respects, survival inverts the value of civilization. Physical existence can no longer be dismissed as unworthy of concern. The body's will and the will of the spirit must join in common cause.
— Terrence Des Pres, *The Survivor*

The great majority of us are required to live a life of constant, systematic duplicity. Your health is bound to be affected if, day after day, you say the opposite of what you feel, if you grovel before what you dislike and rejoice at what brings you nothing but misfortune. Our nervous system isn't just a fiction, it's part of our physical body, and our soul exists in space and is inside us, like the teeth in our mouth. It can't forever be violated with impunity.
— Boris Pasternak, *Doctor Zhivago*

Spring was ushered in, amidst all of its full, heady glory. The tulip bulbs that I had planted with the boys the previous autumn sprouted in radiant splendor. The apple tree in our front yard, with its intoxicating scent, was in full bloom. Even the kids seemed to have sprouted during their months of winter hibernation. They no longer could squeeze their limbs into the lightweight jackets they had fit into so perfectly in the fall. Everyone and everything seemed to be fully alive with every atom of their being . . . with the exception of Danielle.

For some reason, despite the months of "Jewish mothering" and all its ample fare, Danielle seemed to be withering away. Her finely chiseled features were now frail, her voluptuous body was now narrowing to thinness, her cerulean eyes, hollow. I spoke to her one evening, asking if something was bothering her.

"What's bothering me?" she laughed, incongruously, as if to imply, "how can you be missing the point?" "Everything," she said, with a baffled shrug of her shoulders. "Nothing's changed. I'm just taking a vacation from reality here, at your house. I still haven't received any payment from Eric. The lawyers just seem to be jerking me around. I have no prospects of a job. I haven't heard of any definite openings. Even then, there's no guarantee that I'll get it. My whole life is in limbo. Everything is just so tenuous."

The following day I dialed the personnel office of the school system, asking if they knew of any openings for psychologists for the coming year. "As a matter of fact, we just received a retirement notice in the office, this morning," an animated voice on the other end of the line was saying. "Arnie Smith from Area 4 is going to retire after 25 years of service to the school system."

I thanked her, and immediately called Danielle into my office, the adrenaline rushing to my brain. I started talking eagerly, quickly, with her about a strategy for her to land the job, priming her for the interview with all sorts of sample questions she might want to anticipate, my words flowing together in rapid waves, without breaks between the sentences to come up for air.

"And if they ask you what your worst quality is," I said, staring directly past the hollows, and into her clear blue eyes, "For goodness sakes, don't be honest. Tell them your friends all say you're a workaholic. Tell them you're a perfectionist, and never want to leave the office at five."

She thanked me politely, her voice a monotone, her affect, flat. Her ecru wool knit turtleneck blending into her pale complexion, the boundaries between her skin and the eggshell fabric merging together, in an indistinct sallow, yellow blur. I felt as though she wasn't totally there, as I was talking to her. It seemed that the events of the past few months had sapped all the juices out of her spirit. She seemed so bland, so absent, so colorless.

That night, as we were clearing the dinner dishes, Danielle mentioned to me that she would be arriving to work late the following morning, that she had made an appointment with the doctor for a routine physical examination.

Chapter 20

PARTICLES OF LIGHT

And in the evening, when I lie in bed and end my prayers with the words, "I thank you, God, for all that is good and clear and beautiful," I am filled with joy. Then I think about "the good" of going into hiding, of my health, and with my whole being of the "dearness" of Peter, of that which is still embryonic and impressionable and which we neither of us dare to name or touch, of that which will come sometime; live, happiness and of "the beauty" which exists in the world; the world, nature, beauty, and that is exquisite and fine.

I don't think then of all the misery, but of the beauty that still remains. My advice is "Go outside, to the fields, enjoy nature and the sunshine, go out and try to recapture happiness in yourself and in God. Think of the beauty that's still left in and around you and be happy.

— Anne Frank, *The Diary of a Young Girl*

May my heart always be open to little birds who are the secrets
of living whatever they sing is better than to know and if men
should not hear them men are old.
— e.e. cummings

Danielle did not arrive in the office at all the next day. When
I finally saw her, it was late in the evening. The children and
I had already finished dinner. Her absence was very apparent. The brisk bustling and light and spicy conversation of
the kitchen was slowed, muted. As much as I tried to restrain
my impulse to worry, I was feeling heated, tense. The children
picked up on my anxiety, asking where she was. I lied that she
had a late meeting, a home visit, to parents who worked and
couldn't get off from their jobs for a conference concerning
their truant son.

When I finally heard the key in the door and the creaking
of the floorboards as Danielle slowly entered the foyer, my heart
sank. Her eyes were red, swollen. Her hair stringy, disheveled.
The blood had gone from her face. Her pace was sluggish, hesi-
tant, as though she was reluctant to face the group. She carried with her the faint odor of alcohol, something I had never
known her to abuse before.

The kids saw her and dispersed into their own directions,
like little mice into their holes, sensing immediately, with their
child-like, instinctive wisdom, that something was not right,
and that they would be in over their heads if they were around
to learn of it.

We sat down at the kitchen table. I passed a plate in her
direction, motioning with my palm for her to take some salad.
She was giddy, laughing in a kind of whirling daze. She began
speaking in a frivolous, light-headed, semi-coherent manner.
"I couldn't go back to the office, today. It was such a marvelous day. The air was so fresh. I never knew spring could be so

beautiful." She was smiling broadly now. I noticed tiny specks of water, like dew, forming in the little corners of her eyes. "The birds were really busy singing and doing their thing. Do they always sing like that, or was today special for some reason? I can't believe I've been oblivious to them my whole life. I actually saw a cardinal today — he was so vividly red — that's what 'red' really means." She was crying now, in great streams beneath her smile. My arm was around her, instinctively. How long had it been there? I didn't know.

"I just couldn't face another borderline retarded kid drooling on me today. If I would've missed this glorious day to ask another WISC-R question, I would've thrown up." As she continued speaking, I felt her grasp on reality lighten up, or maybe, she was closer to it than most of us usually are.

"I knew it was there all along," she said now, between heaves. "I felt the lump in the shower months ago. I just couldn't focus on it. With the divorce, the house, everything — I just didn't have the energy."

The smile was still there, engraved permanently between sobs, as though to deny the reality of her pain. "He sent me right away for a mammogram. I knew when the technician came back after developing the first film. She was so infernally chipper."

She looked at me directly with those clear blue eyes of hers, now etched with tiny spiders of red in the cornea. "They asked me to wait. They had a radiologist on staff who read the film right away. Isn't modern medicine wonderful? They sent me right back up to Dr. Feinstein who told me. They've scheduled me for a biopsy tomorrow morning."

"But Danielle," I said, "there's a chance it could be benign. You don't know."

"No," she said with that air of certitude of hers which I used to envy, but didn't at the moment, "I know."

End of discussion.

Before we headed upstairs, I held her very close, hugged her very hard, as if to chase away her nightmares. I wished I had a myth, a fairy tale on hand to tell her, to comfort her through the night. I had none.

Everything happened so quickly after that, like the steady stream of lashes from out of a concentration camp guard's whip. Danielle had asked for the application for the position in Area 4, but she never filled out the form, and left it standing there in the pile of unfinished business on my desk, gathering dust. As usual, Danielle's instincts had been borne out. The malignancy had spread to both breasts, requiring a radical bilateral mastectomy.

It was as though all her disappointment and all her illusion had focused themselves upon the fragile cytoplasm and nuclei of the breast tissue. It had metastasized through her blood stream, as though that site had been too narrow to confine all of her anguish into.

It was all so quick and brutal. Dr. Feinstein referred her to Dr. Sugarman, a "first rate" surgeon, who scheduled her for surgery the following Wednesday. They seemed to be racing against a deadly clock, and we knew that they were.

Danielle seemed tightly controlled, stoic. It was almost as though she had expected this for some time, as though the disease came as a welcome relief, on some level, from the angst of her indefinite state, of the uncertainty of her limbo quantum existence.

In this time before the surgery, I often noticed Danielle holding an Artscroll edition of the Book of Psalms. I noticed her one evening, standing alone in the living room, facing east, her posture erect, and reciting in her broken Hebrew:

> *Mizmoor LaDavid*
> *Adonai Roweey Lo Echsur*
> *Binot Desha YiBatzani*
> *Il may minachot yinhalani*

(A Psalm of David, God is my shepherd,
   I shall not lack.
In lush pastures, He makes me lie, besides
   tranquil waters, He leads me.)
Gam key aylech
BiGan tsimahvat
Lo eyree rah eymahdey
(Though I walk in the valley of the shadow
   of death, I will fear no evil
   for You are with me.)

I stood there, frozen, watching her, as her lips strained to make the difficult configurations of the ancient syllables. I felt a different but vaguely familiar emotion registering just then. It was more powerful than simple awe. It was awe, yes, but awe mixed with something else. Was it envy? She had the capacity for such faith. She was cut out of the sweet, simple fabric of a believer. She was able to make that great leap beyond the visual, empirical world. Was I? Did I have the same capacity to respond in such a consoling way, at such a time? I wasn't sure that I had.

When did I last experience that emotion? Of course! It was when I had watched my father standing, fasting, praying, while his body was being consumed by cancer, all day in front of a congregation that last Yom Kippur before he died. Later, afterward, I had called it "a triumph of the human spirit" to him, and he beamed in his silent, secret wisdom.

That was when I first realized that people die exactly as they live. There are no divine revelations that confront you on your death bed, no sudden moments of epiphany. The cranky ones in the nursery are probably the nasty ones in the nursing homes. The cynics live and die as cynics. The faithful live and die in faith. It is not an empirical matter. It is not a matter of science or logic or deduction. It is a matter of faith and feeling and intuition. Whether you have it or not depends more on the kind of cloth that you are cut from, for it is deeply rooted in your psychological being. It depends more on your intuition, on your ability to trust and bond, both to humans and to dimensions outside the human, visible sphere, than upon logic. For the distinction between knowledge and faith is one of belief, or of a trust that extends beyond the empirical universe.

I had sensed that the children had realized that there was something wrong, not by anything they said, but by subtle nuances in their behavior. Nicole began speaking to her mother in softer more deferential tones. The caustic edge to her speech had been totally cut out. Max became the eternal optimist, the wisecracker, the provider of quick, and often hilarious, dead-pan one-liners. He seemed to feel it was his responsibility to buoy the family's spirits. And Leah began to cling to me, developing nightmares, and climbing into my bed at night, although her mother was just downstairs in the living room. Maybe she was afraid to venture down the stairs alone at night, although a night light shone in the hall, but I suspected that it was more than that — that it had something to do with that intuitive wisdom of children, and of her need for a secure and stable maternal bond. It became a nightly ritual for her little footsteps to make their way into my bedroom, and I would move closer to David, as her little, supple body made its way up to our large, king-sized bed. Her auburn hair cascaded across my pillow, always smelling of baby shampoo, and I would be lulled back to sleep, tranquilized by the gentle, rhythmic sound of her breathing.

David assumed his characteristic posture as the Rock of Gibraltar, always available to Danielle for midnight medical consultations, calling colleagues to check out the reputations of her doctors, staying up nights moonlighting at the N.I.H. library, reading everything that was ever written about breast cancer and about the various alternative treatments, calling every medical expert in the field, from all around the world, at Harvard, at Mt. Sinai, at Johns Hopkins, at U.C.L.A., at Oxford and Cambridge. They all had something different to say. He knew that Danielle was depending on his advice in deciding what to do if the surgery wasn't totally successful. To her, he appeared confident, optimistic, upbeat. But internally, he was a conflicted mass of confusion. It was not an enviable position to be in.

And I, characteristically, was feeling angry and abandoned. What was going on here? Was God playing some sort of cruel, practical joke on me? Why was it that almost every person I loved was being ripped out of my picture? My father, my mother, who was there only in body, and not in mind, Rivka, and now Danielle? I almost felt like a carrier of some sort of deadly virus, like putting myself in some sort of affective quarantine, wearing a "Beware of Entry" sign across my chest, isolating myself and protecting innocent and unsuspecting victims from the brutal effects of my heart. I could just picture it, in bold letters. "Warning: The Surgeon General of the United States Advises that Entry into the Chambers May Pose a Serious Risk to Your Health." It was true. It seemed like anyone who received my affection and found his way into my heart's lethal chambers ran the definite risk of a shortened life expectancy.

One night, after the children had been tucked into their beds, I spoke candidly to Danielle about it. We were alone in the kitchen, sharing our nightly pot of tea.

"I'm so angry at everyone, at God, really. Why is He doing this to you?"

"Why?" she said, half-stunned.

"You're so young. You've gone through so much this past year. Too much for one person. You're trying so hard to be a good Jew. You don't deserve this.

She put her arm around my shoulder, as if to console me. "Why bother with your anger? I don't feel that way. Why should you?"

"But, do you ever think, why is God doing this to you?"

"I don't believe that God is punishing me. I can't . . . I can't believe God is that vindictive. I don't believe He controls every little virus that invades every little organ. I think His scope is much larger than that. I'm at peace, Rach. Why can't you be?"

I listened intently to her words. They were beginning to penetrate through my thick, cynical skin. I wasn't able to fall asleep until after I heard the soft, nimble patter of Leah's footsteps, and felt the warmth of her body in her pink flannel nightgown, sleeping peacefully next to mine.

Chapter 21

LUMINESCENCE

He who finds a thought that lets us penetrate
even a little deeper into the eternal mystery of
nature has been granted great grace.
— Albert Einstein

In the end he has nothing, nothing at all but this short reprieve,
this extra life free and his own. The loss of particular hope opens
on the power of life in itself, something unexpected, uncovered
when the spirit is driven down to its roots and through its pain
is brought to a stillness and finality which — as men once said
— surpasses understanding. For survivors that is enough.
— Terrence Des Pres, *The Survivor*

Wednesday morning. Danielle packed a few additional items
into her beige and mauve tweed tote bag: her nightgown, her
toothbrush, her makeup, her book of Tehillim, of the Psalms of
David.

We left early for Georgetown University Hospital. The sun's rays bathed Rock Creek Parkway in an incandescent pink glow. There was very little conversation in the car. David stared directly ahead at the early morning commuter traffic. Danielle gazed stoically out the window, occasionally groping inside her tote bag to check that the Book of Psalms was still there.

The operation was long — five hours. David had rescheduled his morning patients, but had to go back to the hospital after a few hours. He left me alone in the lobby, waiting, waiting, waiting. Why do hospitals always smell so heavily of Parson's ammonia — as if to camouflage the scent of the emission of bodily fluids, as if to conceal the events behind those closed metal doors?

There were a few worn copies of ladies' magazines on a coffee table. I picked them up as if to read them, but I knew I couldn't. My mind was tense, racing like a tightly wound top. I looked up and glanced at the crucifix suspended on the wall there, the symbol of one Jewish martyr who had died almost two thousand years ago which Danielle had traded in for that of six million Jewish martyrs who had died 40 years ago. What did it matter — whichever would give comfort to a troubled soul?

It was then that I found myself in the middle of the abyss, wishing I had Danielle's copy of the Book of Psalms, a crucifix, a Holy Grail, something — anything to clutch onto to give me faith. Instead, I found myself staring right past the crucifix on the wall, internally, to the image of the grandparents I never knew, engraved in my memory, crying, praying silently inside: "Please Bubbie, Zadie. She did not ask to have her seeds planted in hostile soil. Please spare this poor soul, whose storm-scattered fate was not of her design. Please. Please. Give her life. *VeShivtow LeBet HaShem LaOrach Yamim.* So that she may dwell in the house of God for long days."

I looked up, startled. A sound had emitted from my lips. What was I saying? Were these ancient Hebrew words of King David coming from my lips, me, who had always found it so difficult to pray? I recognized the words. They were at the end of the 23rd Psalm — Danielle's favorite. What had this person done to me? Given me?

She was wheeled back from the recovery room and lifted onto the bed, so waif-like, so pale. The heavy, thick wrapping of the white tape across her chest showing through her flimsy aqua hospital gown. She was groggy, half conscious, her body heavily anesthetized, the smell of drugs emanating from her.

Suddenly, she tried to lift her head from the pillow, and asked me for her tote bag. I gave it to her. Her hand reached into it. I had expected her to pull out the Book of Psalms. Instead she pulled out an old picture of a handsome young man, in a tarnished sterling silver frame, looking valiant and regal in the uniform of the Waffen SS.

"Vater, Vater," she said, in her half-dream like state, *"Ich lieben Sie. Ich lieben Sie."*

Chapter 22

Quantum Leaps

We are rarely aware of the gravitational forces we embody
for others, but we are keenly aware of the gravitational
forces certain others embody for us. To say "my father,"
"my mother," is for me to name but in no way to ap-
proach one of the central mysteries of my life. . . .
All children mythologize their parents, who are to them,
after all, giants of the landscape of early childhood.
— Joyce Carol Oates, *My Father, My Fiction*

I came to the hospital early the following morning. She recoiled
from my face, turning her head away from mine in the most profound sort of disgust that only self-shame can evoke, only the sort
one feels after having disclosed some deep, dark family secret.

"What are you doing here?" she said, with more than just a
slight edge of hostility to her voice, as though I was a stranger,
an intruder of sorts — maybe I was.

"You just had major surgery, Danielle. You *are* my friend, you know."

There she was, lying there in that bed, which suddenly seemed so large for her now shrunken, frail body, so pathetic, so pale, trying so desperately to defend what little was left of her dignity. She suddenly reminded me of a little sparrow with clipped wings, trying to fly. She's been stripped of so much — her husband, her wealth, her status, her security . . . and now, suddenly, in one fell swoop . . . her breasts . . . and her myths.

She was crying now. She turned her head away from mine, and stared out the window.

"It's all right, Danielle. It's all right." I said, stroking her hair off of her face.

"What's all right?" She turned toward me with bitterness. "Nothing is all right. Everything is awful."

She was crying more now. I reached for a tissue from off the night stand, and began wiping the tear stains from her cheeks, which seemed to drip down in streams like little streaks of rain across a window pane.

"I know. I know. It's okay, baby. It doesn't matter."

"What doesn't matter?"

"About your dad. I know, honey. I've known for a long time," I said, still trying to dab away those little wet streaks on her face. The flow wouldn't stop.

She turned to me, startled. "When did you know? How long have you known?"

"It doesn't matter."

"No . . . tell me . . . I have to know."

"Well, ever since that first time you had me over to the house in Georgetown."

"God. That seems like so long ago. It seems like another lifetime away. " Still more tears.

"And . . . how could you? How could you be so nice to me? Knowing what you know?" There was that edge of hostility, again.

"It doesn't matter, honey. You were not a Nazi. You're not responsible for the sins of your father. You're just not. You're your own person, Danielle. It isn't your fault, honey. It just isn't your fault."

She looked at me incredulously, her mouth half opened to breath in some air. I kept dabbing away those tear streaks, which kept dripping down in a steady stream.

"And besides," I continued, "he's dead. The war is over — and he is dead and buried."

She tried to lift her body from the bed. "Dead? Whoever said anything about dead?"

"You did, always. You've always told me he's dead."

"I said a lot of things about him which weren't totally true."

"You mean he's alive?"

She nodded.

"That's impossible!"

"How do you know? Do you know something I don't know, Rach?"

"No. It's just that I know his file at the Justice Department is stamped 'inactive.' "

"I can't believe you know all that." She turned away, again, in disgust.

"But why is that. If he's alive?"

"Because he ratted. He informed on his friends. That's the least of his sins. He helped gather evidence for the government for the Ivan Demjanjuk Trial and the Klaus Barbie trial through his contacts. The government granted him immunity from prosecution."

"I can't believe it! Where is he?"

"First he flew to Paraguay. But now he lives in Brazil. In Rio . . . Rio de Janeiro."

"But you never talked to him. You never wrote. He might have been able to help you through all of this these past few months."

She cut me off, quickly. "No. As far as I'm concerned, he's been dead for a long, long time. The father I loved as a little girl died for me, slowly, when the truth about him began to gradually unfold about his Nazi past."

"But Danielle. You loved him. You still do. I saw you holding that picture, yesterday."

"No." She interrupted me, again. "That was not the father I loved. That was another man — a murderer."

"And your mother? What about your mother?"

"As far as I'm concerned, she's worse than he is. Always trying to protect him. Always trying to cover things up, and sweep them under the rug. Like some mindless little Pollyanna."

"Where is she living?"

"She's with him in Rio. I'm sure they're living a very comfortable life, there."

So that explained it! The wealth, that seemed to have so abruptly disappeared from this family, which could have been so useful these past months to this daughter who was nearly destitute.

"Danielle, don't you think. . . . They should know, I mean about your illness, you know. . . ."

"Don't bother." She cut me off, again. "As far as they were concerned, I died a long time ago. I committed the equivalent of murder in their eyes when I married Eric. They used to call him 'that Semitic swine.' And I was 'the bleeding heart American liberal' whose life had been 'too cushy to really understand anything about life.' We've had nothing to do with each other for years."

"But Danielle, how do you know about their whereabouts?"

"I get an occasional letter from Uncle Bruno in Berlin, pleading with me to ask them for forgiveness and make peace."

"But don't you think, now that you're sick and everything. . . . You might want to. . . . Maybe Uncle Bruno is right?"

"Are you crazy, Rach? 'Me' ask 'them' for forgiveness. I'm not responsible for anyone's death. You said that yourself, just a few moments ago."

"But maybe now, you might want to make peace with them?"

"Don't waste your breath, Rach. They hated me the moment I stopped being their 'sweet little, blond Dresden doll' and started thinking for myself. They used to call me 'the Ugly American' when I could no longer swallow their myths and started asking questions that made them feel a little uncomfortable."

"But. . . ."

"But nothing, Rach. I've been dead to them for years . . . and they have to me."

Subject closed — or so she thought.

Chapter 23

TENUOUS
EQUILIBRIUM

That corpse you planted last year in your garden.
Has it begun to sprout? Will it bloom this year? Or
has the sudden frost disturbed its bed?
— T.S. Eliot, *The Waste Land*

That's the difficulty in these times: ideals, dreams,
and cherished hopes rise within us, only to meet
the horrible truth and be shattered.
— Anne Frank, *The Diary of a Young Girl*

Summer set in. The children spent long evenings chasing
fireflies, and collecting them in old coffee jars, making little
punctures on the top with kitchen knives so that they could get
air to breath. Their bodies had become brown and slender from
all the swimming and sun. Max was spending a lot of time with
David, and had taken to reading Spinoza and Martin Buber.
Nicole was barely around. She had become quite popular with
the boys, and was always rushing off to this disco or that movie.

One of them was a photographer, and was helping her develop a portfolio of pictures of herself.

Danielle and I spent long evenings on the patio together, sipping iced tea, with little mint leaves picked from the garden floating in it, watching the children running after the fireflies or rolling down the grassy hill.

Danielle seemed to be doing fairly well on the chemotherapy, although she was experiencing many of the secondary effects: the hair loss, the nausea.

She was fitted for a prosthesis, which she always wore.

Despite the notorious Washingtonian weather in the summer, she never ventured into the pool. She was afraid her prosthesis might "float away" from her in the water.

Together, we made the trip to Megan's Scandinavian Hair Salon in Wheaton, where we picked out a very natural looking wig, made up "entirely of human hair" as Megan told us with her Brooklyn-Swedish accent.

When Danielle wore her prosthesis, her wig, and her blush, she almost looked like herself again. But to those of us who knew her former radiant self, the underlying frailness and pallor still showed through.

The application for the position opening in Area 4 still remained in the same place on my desk. I noticed that the first line had been filled in with her name (a healthy sign?), but not much else.

Danielle still often carried her copy of the Psalms of David, but I noticed that she also checked some books out of the library on holistic medicine, organic foods, and the natural way to healing. She announced one day in the kitchen that she was going to go on a macrobiotic diet. We all understood, giving her sympathetic little nods of tacit approval, and all began consuming more brown rice and tofu.

One day she came in, announcing she had found out about a macrobiotic retreat, and she planned to go.

A few days later she returned, elated, on a high. She began talking rapidly, excitedly. I actually thought she might become well again.

"Rach, Rach. I can't wait to tell you what happened." She sounded like a sweet 16.

"What?"

"There was this young man, there. He was adorable. A yuppie-lawyer. You know the type — wavy, sandy-brown hair, tortoise shell glasses, khaki pants, docksiders, Ralph Lauren cotton plaid shirts and all. Well, he really was interested in me."

"What happened?'

"One night we took a long walk. It was wonderful. So natural. I felt so young. Anyway, he seemed to want to see me again."

"Oh, Danielle. How nice."

"This has been the first time in years that a man has actually . . . you know, looked at me in that way, you know."

"Well? What happened?" I found myself secretly wishing that something had. I wanted so much for her to have a little remission from all this pain and suffering, one last chance, maybe, at happiness.

She looked at me, and laughed. "What do you mean, 'what happened? Of course nothing happened! What was I going to do — invite him up to my room, and then we would get to talking, and then he would kiss me, and then . . . then what?"

"What do you mean?"

"Then we would kiss, and one thing would lead to another. And then I would take off my prosthesis, and then my wig, and then my make-up . . . by the time I would be finished, he would be out the door, throwing up!" She was laughing, but those little beads of water were beginning to form in the cracks of her eyes, again, underneath her smile.

"And besides," she continued, "I could never get involved with him. He's not Jewish."

Oh, Danielle. My poor little Danielle.

One July afternoon, Danielle returned from her oncologist with that look of horror in her eyes. She told me that her blood platelet count had been dropping, that she needed to be transfused immediately. I knew the time was growing near.

She spent the next afternoon in Georgetown University Hospital getting transfused. The unit she was in had been as pleasant as possible. She had the transfusion on a leather chase lounge chair with magazines at her side, and a TV in the room.

When she returned from the hospital, she seemed spry and full of energy, with what she called "new blood flowing through my veins." I knew the time had come to do what I had to do. That it might be my only time.

I told her that I had some leave time coming to me, and that I badly needed a vacation, that I had to visit my sister in Israel for just a few days . . . that I missed her very badly, and was concerned for her. I asked if she and David could watch the kids. They both agreed.

Danielle drove me over to the El Al Terminal at the airport, hugged me goodbye, and told me not to worry about David or the kids. Everything would be fine. After she left, I took a cab over to Varig Terminal, and boarded a plane headed for Rio de Janeiro.

Chapter 24

Natural Quirks

My story is a story of very ordinary people during extraordinarily terrible times. Times the like of which I hope with all my heart will never, never come again. It is for all of us ordinary people all over the world to see to it that they do not.
— Miep Gies, *Anne Frank Remembered*

Once on the plane, I needed a few stiff drinks to try and settle my nerves. What was I getting myself into? I was terrified. This was the closest I had ever come to meeting a real Nazi before, to coming face to face with real evil. The flight seemed interminably long. Was I out of my mind? I closed my eyes and pictured a man with a whip and brown boots and a brown leather shirt. But I knew I had to do this.

We landed in the airport in Rio. As soon as I passed through customs, a policeman approached me. What had I done?

"Cruzados. You want Cruzados?" He said in his thick Portuguese accent.

What a hospitable country, I thought to myself, but only for a moment. He gave me a police escort to the elevator and upstairs to the official money changing station (at the government rate). The policeman and the clerk behind the counter said a few words together in Portuguese, looked me over and exchanged laughter at some inside joke (probably at my expense). I exchanged a hundred dollars.

"Only a hundred dollars? How long you stay in Brazil?"

"Just overnight."

They looked disappointed, gave me the hundred dollars, and left me to fend for myself. *Welcome to South America*, I thought to myself. *Welcome to the corruption of the Third World. Desperate situations.*

I picked up my suitcase, and looked for a phone book.

There was one, right next to the Hertz Rent-a-Car Counter. I looked first through the Vs . . . Von Himmel . . . Von Hoffmann. There it was! No need to Anglicize it here, I guess.

111 Ipanema.

I hailed a cab. I thought I had experienced terror in the plane, that is, until I had experienced how the Cariocas, the natives of Rio de Janeiro, drove. There were no lanes on the highway. No need for that, no one would drive in them anyway. People just wove in and out, at almost full velocity, racing with one another, as though we were on a speedway.

He looked at me through his rearview mirror.

"American?"

I nodded.

"I am a Cariocas," he said, with pride. "We Cariocas, we the ones who know how to enjoy life. Work? Just enough to get by. In Rio, we have the Corpus Christi. The statue of the

Christ with his hands outstretched. In Sao Paolo they say that the Christ's hands are out there waiting for us to start working. Then he clap!" He closed his eyes and laughed, obviously enjoying his own humor. For my part, I wished he would stop being so sociable, and pay more attention to the road.

We passed through a slum section in Rio, the likes of which I had never seen before in my life. Little children wearing rags. Ladies in brazen red wigs and tight skimpy dresses that looked more like belts than dresses to me, parading their wares. People bathing in public fountains. Little scraps of sheet metal hastily welded together to make their homes.

The taxi sped along a highway, and under an underpass, and finally arrived at the coastal section of Rio de Janeiro I understood immediately why Rio is considered one of the most beautiful cities in the world. The rugged chain of the Serra do Mar mountain peaks came into view, plunging directly into the Bay of Guanabara. In the bay protruded the magnificent Sugar Loaf Mountain and the tiny chain of accompanying islands. On the mountain stood the statue of Christ, just as the taxi driver had described, with his hands outstretched over the city. Along the road was the famous Copacabana Beach. Women of all shapes and sizes were on the beach, scantily clothed with what looked like flimsy excuses for bathing suits, playing volleyball or buying little baubles from a *camelos*, a street vendor. The music of a samba band drifted in the air.

The taxi stopped at 111 Ipanema, a magnificent white marble building, with little green bushes planted in white marble planters, a green and white striped awning, and a very officious looking doorman with a pasted-on smile and a pallor to match the awning at the entrance.

I paid the taxi driver, and the doorman opened the door. Terror is not quite strong enough a word for what I felt at that moment. My heart was pounding almost audibly as I got out of the cab and slowly walked up the entrance way to the building. Here I was, coming face to face with a real Nazi, the embodiment of everything I had ever known to be evil incarnate. Would he recognize me as one who got away, and whisk me off, on a train headed somewhere? Would he tell me to go to the right? Would he look like a monster, a madman?

I asked the doorman to buzz Wilhelm Von Hoffmann. He asked who I was, and I told him Rachel Stein, a friend of his daughter's. There was a little conversation in Portuguese across the switchboard. The doorman eyed me again, not without some suspicion, and said, "Who?" I repeated myself, knowing almost immediately I should have assumed an alias, something not quite so obviously Jewish.

There was a little more discussion across the switchboard wires, and then the doorman reluctantly told me that he was in apartment 1711, and showed me to the elevator.

The elevator was so slow! I finally made it to the 17th floor, and found my way to his apartment.

With sweaty hands, I rang his doorbell.

A tall, distinguished, man opened the door, and shook my hand. *"Bom dia,"* he said. "Won't you come in?"

Mozart's "Piano Concerto #21 in C" was on the stereo. A sweet-looking gray-haired lady was putting red poppies in a vase, bustling about in the background, arranging things. The apartment was tastefully furnished with European antiques, a baby grand piano, and Persian rugs. A beautiful vista of the bay and the mountains showed through the windows. He asked me to sit down. "Tell me," he said, "what brings you to Brazil?"

"I've come about your daughter, Danielle."

He looked concerned for a minute, while I continued. "She's sick. It's cancer . . . breast cancer. I thought you should know."

A look of profound pain crossed his face. "Danielle," he said, "Danielle," as if evoking old memories.

His wife came out of the background, her eyes etched with agony. She opened her mouth as if to say something, but then immediately looked at her husband and kept her mouth tightly locked, as if it had actually been physically muzzled shut.

Then, Mr. Von Hoffmann spoke: "Danielle who?"

"Your daughter, Danielle Schoenfeld."

"Danielle Schoenfeld?" he said slowly, as if he didn't recognize the name. "I'm sorry. You must be mistaken. I knew of a Danielle Von Hoffmann once. But a Danielle Schoenfeld? I'm terribly sorry. You must have the wrong person."

He got up, as if to escort me out the door. As he was about to close it, he studied my eyes intently, and said to me, in a half-whisper, "Tell her . . . I'm sorry." Then he quickly shut the door.

The flight back seemed to go much quicker than the flight there. Danielle had been right about him, I thought to myself, as she had been about so much. Exhausted, I drifted off to sleep.

Chapter 25

INFINITE UNIVERSES

One day, I was running an errand and I found myself
in the ghetto. There were all kinds of people, pregnant
women, children screaming, "Mama, Mama!" Then I saw
a woman with an infant in her arms. With one movement
of his hand, the SS man pulled the baby away and threw
it to the ground. I could not understand. But later on I
realized that God gave us free will to be good or bad. So
I asked God for forgiveness, and said if the opportunity
arrived I would help these people.
— Irene Gut Opdyke, quoted in
Rescuers: Portraits of Moral Courage in the Holocaust
by Gay Block and Malka Drucker

I hadn't been home for more than 24 hours when an aerogram
from Israel arrived in the neat, careful handwriting I immediately recognized as Rivka's. I quickly ripped it open.

Dearest Rachel,

I want to put your mind at ease, my dear little sister.
I hope my last letter didn't trouble you too much. That
was not at all my intention. Things seem, for the time
being, to be really holding steady, *"Baruch HaShem."*
My white blood cell count, thank God, is fine.

Every week, I have to cross over the "green line"
from the territories for my radiation and chemotherapy
treatments into Jerusalem to Hadassah Hospital in
Kiryat Yovel. The journey is very frightening to me.
Each time, rocks are thrown, glass is shattered, and windows are replaced, only to be shattered again. Very few
people venture out of the territories, unless absolutely
necessary. When I have to do it, I find myself actually
shivering (physically) with fear. I find myself reciting the
Tefillat HaDarech with renewed conviction and cavanah.
(I guess that's what they mean by the old expression
that there are no atheists in the trenches.) Somehow, I
always feel renewed when I enter the hills of Jerusalem
to the *Mercaz HaMercazit*, the central bus station, where
I change buses to Kiryat Yovel. Something about those
green hills is so calming, so comforting, in an almost
magical way. I could almost picture David Hamelech
himself, standing there with his sheep, playing on his
harp. (Maybe it's just the sheer sense of relief that I've
survived the journey, but sometimes, I think it's something more.)

Something very strange happened to me last week.
I know you'll understand when I tell it to you, but I'm
afraid not everyone would. I was particularly frightened
of this journey because I couldn't find anyone to watch
Amir, whose *gan* [kindergarten] was closed for teacher
conferences. Elonals *matapalat* [baby sitter], has a new
baby, and between her baby and Elona, she already has
her hands full. (As you know, Elona can be a handful by

herself.) I could usually count on my neighbor, Norit, in a pinch, but her mother has not been well and she is in Petach Tikvah taking care of her. I just couldn't see any alternative but to take Amir with me. Despite my worst fears, there was only one rock-throwing incident, and Thank God, no-one was hurt. Just the usual shattering of glass.

The waiting room was particularly full at the radiation/chemotherapy section of Hadassah. (So much cancer for such a tiny country. That too, with everything else it has to contend with.) It was filled with the usual assortment of Israeli *tiposim* [types]. All sorts of people in their assigned costumes. Arab men in their jeans and *kafiyahs*, or Arab women in their shawls and black, embroidered dresses. Chasidic men in their black hats and long, black coats or Chasidic women in their long dresses, white stockings, and *shetles*. Yemenite women with their dark features and bright dresses. Modern Orthodox Jews in their jeans and *Kipot serugot* [knitted *yarmulkas*]. Secular Jews with half-unbuttoned shirts, golden stars dangling from chains around their necks, and tightly fitting Jordache jeans.

You know, as a mother, how whenever you travel anywhere you pack along some of the kids' favorite treats and toys to keep them occupied? Well, Amir was on the floor, underfoot of everybody, playing with his marbles (his latest favorite toy). A little Arab boy with short, dark hair and a turquoise shirt, sat down on the floor and started playing with him. They started shooting the marbles, which Fa'ad called *"tuwab"* [balls], in an imaginary sphere. I don't know what it was. Maybe it was that they were intrigued by the bright colors of the little glass balls. Maybe it was that they would die of boredom if the didn't have each other and those marbles. But they were able to understand each other.

Together, in their crazy amalgam of Arabic and Hebrew, they constructed intricate rules of their little game, and played together so nicely.

When Fa'ad's mother was called in to see the doctor, he started crying for her. I glanced at her understandingly, and said *"Yelodim"* ["children" in Hebrew]. She returned my glance and shrugged *"Awlad"* ["children" in Arabic]. I told her, in Hebrew, that I would watch him while she was being treated. She smiled at me, cautiously, and told me she would do the same for me.

Fa'ad was still crying, as she was going into the room. I held him in my lap, talking to him as I would to Amir, only in my pigeon-Arabic, saying *"Waqqaf baka"* [stop crying], that *"umm"* [mother] will be back soon. Just before entering the room, his mother flashed us a look of pain that stabbed me to the core with her deep, dark eyes. It was a stab of familiarity. It was that look of a real fear. Of a fear I know so well of having to leave a crying child, without being able to comfort him. Not just for now, but possibly forever.

That's when it hit me just how insane this Arab/Jew thing really is. It's like their game of marbles. While you're inside the sphere it's so meaningful with its intricate little rules. Which little glass ball is worth more because of its color or clarity. But once you step out of the sphere, it's totally meaningless.

I just don't have the strength to fight that sort of battle, anymore. Maybe it's because I'm too tired. But maybe it's because my illness has taught me what's really important in life. I just want to live, and to be there to watch my children grow up. And I want them to be able to live out full, rich lives, rather than to have to face each other in the battlefield over someone else's rules of the little game, like their game of marbles. I wonder if Fa'ad's mother is having the same feeling. I bet a lot of mothers, deep down inside, are. Secretly, at least.

Please send Benyamen and Joshua great big hugs and kisses from their favorite (and only) aunt. Best regards to David.

Love forever,

Rivka

I carefully folded the letter and put it upstairs in my night table drawer right next to my bed, where I knew it would be safe. And where I knew I could always find it when I felt I needed a reminder of what it means to be human.

Chapter 26

MYSTIC CONSTANTS

We have to admire in humility the beautiful harmony of the structure of this world, as far as we can grasp it. That is all.
— Albert Einstein

Late August. Danielle's blood platelet count was steadily dropping. Her doctor called her in for another transfusion, but this time he wanted her to pack her bags.

We arrived at the hospital. She was gripping tightly onto her copy of Tehillim, the Psalms, reciting the words over and over again in her broken Hebrew. We knew the end was near.

She was losing her appetite. The hospital nurses brought her trays of vegetarian food, but she couldn't eat it. Her cheeks got more and more sunken, her body progressively smaller and smaller, in what seemed to be that increasingly large hospital bed. She seemed to be quickly fading away.

In the end, she was drifting in and out of consciousness. The doctors had a term for it, "semi-comatose," which we all know means being tenuously suspended somewhere above that fragile abyss between the world we know about, and the one which we fear.

I was with her at the end. She was clutching on to my hand, with her frail little fingers, like that of a newborn. Her eyes were so big. Hollow. "The children . . . the children," she moaned, over and over again, as if to say, "My work isn't really finished here yet. The children."

"Don't worry about the children. Don't worry, honey, they're in good hands."

She seemed to come out of her coma for a moment. "Rach," she said, "Max and Nicole are almost grown, but Leah . . . Leah. Can she be the daughter you've always longed for?"

"Of course she can."

She closed her eyes, seeming to be at peace. "Rach, thank you. You have given me so much. What is it that I have ever given you?"

"A lot more than I ever gave you. What a gift you have given me, Danielle! You have given me my faith."

She smiled to herself and closed her eyes at that, to what I knew to have been the final time, and drifted off to a peaceful sleep. I slipped the open book of Tehillim from off the night stand, and continued reading from where she had left off.

"Adonai roweey low echtsur."

" God is my shepherd, I shall not want."

Chapter 27

TOWARD A UNIFIED FIELD THEORY

Our only hope will lie in the frail web of
understanding of one person for the pain of another.
— John Dos Passos

The sun was scorching hot at the cemetery, the day of the funeral. The children and I huddled together in a tight web to shield ourselves from the glaring light of the sun, and from the sight of Danielle's sweet body being lowered down into that cold, cold ground. Leah nuzzled her head into my chest to block out the sight. We all did the best we could to keep from breaking down.

Somewhere in the background, a rabbi was saying the words, *"Yis Gadal ViYiskAddash Shmay Rabah."* David was helping to lift the cold soil up and shovel it over the grave.

Leah crawled into bed with me from the start that night. The window was open, and from outside we had a clear vista of the summer sky, with its radiantly shining stars.

"Rachel," Leah said, her slender little body turned toward the opened window, "do you see that star up there? The one that's shining so brightly?"

"Yeah, honey?" I turned and looked at what she was pointing to — what I knew to be the North Star.

"Well, I think that's my mommy up there, trying to talk to us. Maybe she's saying goodbye."

"You're right, sweetheart. You're right," I said, saying the words that I knew would help her to drift off to a peaceful night's sleep. "I'm sure that's your mommy up there, saying goodbye."

EPILOGUE

Rivka is still in remission, and doing very well. The doctors feel her prognosis is very positive. She and her husband are moving back "within the green line," because the weekly trek through the territories to Hadassah Hospital in Jerusalem has become a nightmare of terror for her. As Rivka put it, "Hanging on to life is enough of a struggle — hanging on to life there is just a bit too much." The continuous shattering of glass of their windshield has worked to shatter their hopes into dozens of fragile splinters, refracting in the sunlight into clusters of slender, tiny illusory fragments. The prisms formed by these cut glass pieces can be tempting to look at, seductive in their radiance from afar, but that beauty masks the sharp, jagged edges of their underlying reality. Get to close and one can easily find himself trapped within the lethal dynamic of their trajectory.

Nicole is still working on her portfolio. She is planning to send it to the Ford Modeling Agency in New York when she finishes high school.

Max is going to be Bar Mitzvahed in our synagogue in the fall. He is planning on enrolling in a Yeshiva in Israel after he finishes high school where he can "carry on the dream."

And Leah is now enrolled in the same school where we send our boys, where she is making a good adjustment. She always wears her mother's 24-karat gold Star of David around her neck, which she calls "her most cherished item."